AS BIG AS THE RITZ

GREGORY BENFORD

an imprint of

ARC MANOR

Rockville, Maryland

ISBN: 978-1-61242-316-6

www.PhoenixPick.com
Great Science Fiction & Fantasy
Free Ebook Every Month

Published by Phoenix Pick
an imprint of Arc Manor
P. O. Box 10339
Rockville, MD 20849-0339
www.ArcManor.com

It is youth's felicity as well as its insufficiency that it can never live in the present, but must always be measuring up the day against its own radiantly imagined future—flowers and gold, girls and stars, they are only prefigurations and prophecies of that incomparable, unattainable young dream.
—F. Scott Fitzgerald
"The Diamond as Big as the Ritz," 1922

Kings and fools
Make their own rules.
—Joan Abbe

1.

A lingering respect for the niceties of an Earthside education was the bane of the asteroid communities. Yearly it drained them of their brightest young men and women.

Thus the parents of Clayton Donner persistently pressured him to attend Harvard or Cambridge or Tokyo General, picking these names from a list as unfathomable as a menu in Swahili. Each locale was pictured in verdant 3D as a cultured pinnacle, a doorway to a different life.

The asteroids had been colonized by those who respected no conventional wisdoms but instead made their own. Those ancestors, now in their vacuum-dried graves, would have wrinkled their noses at the odor of flatlander-envy that pervaded the discussions of Clayton's destiny. The boy was quick, studious, clever. He would have made a fine metal-ceramics man, bio-integrater or snytho-miner. Instead, his parents relentlessly pressured him into an Earthside education extracted from books rather than from the gray tumbling worlds.

After his first year flatside Clayton was a convert to their cause. For a young man a career is a distant, fuzzy goal. Earth was concrete and *fun*. Gaudy. Effervescent. Deliciously lurid.

A banquet, topped off by the chemical consolations of civilization. He visited what was left of Africa, sampled the original abode where men had evolved, and came away with both a skin rash and a faint incredulity that anything worthwhile could have started there.

The east coast of the Americas was rather better, though clearly past its great days. The focus of Earthside economic life had shifted to the pan-Pacific nations over a century before. The snug, smug eastern streets were steeped in murky history and claustrophobic assumptions. Clayton stayed in the Ritz-Carlton hotel in Boston, spending a week's worth of his father's profits in two days. The building was well preserved, eccentric by modern standards, and impressed him deeply with its timeless gilded swank. He tasted the now-rare lobster and savored the heady fragrances of orderly decline. A woman he met in the bar seemed to find his asteroid origins fascinating, exotic, and within a few hours she was in his bed. It was a perfect setting to lose his virginity. He was only mildly disturbed when, the next morning, she firmly showed him the Greater Boston price sheet and luxury tax scale. He irritably paid up, resolving that the experience would not blemish his memory of the Ritz and its majesty.

He had ended up at UCLA, his ability and personality profile matched with the school's needs and strengths by an elaborate trait-sifting program; the education of the young was too important to be left to their vagrant tastes.

Like virtually everyone's, his life appeared dull from the outside, or at best made of elements from a soap opera, while from inside it had all the sweep and grandeur of *War and Peace*. Clayton went through the usual undergraduate crises. He learned to conceal his naive assumptions and be shocked at nothing. Fashion allowed one to be occasionally stunned, but only within severe limits. Dismay, however, was his for the asking; it implied a certain haughty despair. He tried the various exploits—sexual, social, hallucinogenic—appropriate to his age. Struggling, he invested ideas from survey courses, earnest late-night bull sessions, Op-Ed pages and other fast-thought franchises. He imagined that he was crossing new frontiers, when in fact he was only crossing into Iowa; billions had been there before. He did not suspect that a decade later he would find these pulse-quickening reaches not a little boring.

In his second year he met Sylvia. She was different from the other students—intent, dedicated, severe. Her devotion to the cause of selfless politics was already well known at UCLA. He was mildly attracted to her, despite her habit of wearing loose-fitting, dowdy attire in dull browns and grays.

She was known as Sylvia Hammersmith at UCLA, but that meant little—at that time students often adopted the names of famous people as a gesture. As the young grew more and more alike, devices to distinguish themselves became ever more enticing. Sylvia's taking the name of an explorer, fatally crushed on Venus the year before, seemed only a mild affection.

When he discovered her true last name, however, his interest deepened. Compared to any savvy Earthy, Clayton was still downright naive. Still, he sized up Sylvia quickly and judged his best approach. She wore a perpetual frown, assaying even casual remarks for their moral gold, so—intuiting rapidly—he decided to not mention his major subject of study, Comparative Astrophysics. Instead, he talked endlessly of his minor area, Analytic Economic Morality.

He was, without thinking about it very much, solidly for Earthside's social shibboleths of the era—strict equality of pay for all, abolishment of all inherited wealth right down to items of clothing and furniture, and numerous measures to alleviate any trace of economic envy. The university incorporated these ideas as best it could, but found difficulty staffing the scientific fields, since technical talent could easily find work elsewhere. Support for progressive ideas centered, naturally enough, among the professoriate devoted to such subjects as Greek pottery and interpersonal dynamics.

These notions met with Sylvia's approval, and she opened up a bit. He learned of her laughing, pouting mouth, her glinting sea-blue eyes, her natural and unstudied grace. Quickly he became entranced. He was a man of the world now; certain mature delights should naturally come his way.

All the same, he was amazed when she invited him to spend December at her father's. Though this might be customary if she lived on Earth, or even in one of the crystalline orbital cities, she casually revealed that she was Sylvia Townsworth Rollan. Her father was founder of the most bizarre enterprise in the solar system: Brother-world. It orbited at a steep tilt to the ecliptic, about two astronomical units away from the sun. Getting there would have taken expensive weeks by conventional transport.

Until this moment his interest in Sylvia had largely centered upon the pure, pointed lust of a young man. Mores of other era had swung back to a constraining reticence in matters sexual. Clayton was well socialized, and believed various unsupported assertions that had the effect of delaying marriage, postponing children and generally defusing the explosive power of adolescent sexuality. Sublimation is a subtle game, one the twenty-second played well. His warmly remembered night in the Ritz now seemed to be a gauzy treat, unreal, like cotton candy at a circus.

Ambition he had a-plenty. After Sylvia's invitation he went immediately to his Major Tutor and asked advice. The gray-haired woman listened attentively, then said flatly that he must go, of course. There was no question. It could make his career.

Clayton was slightly shocked to find his own secret thoughts so freely voiced. He observed a quickening in the Major tutor's manner, a fine-drawn anticipation of possible benefits to herself. Clayton remarked that he was reluctant to mix his regard for Sylvia and his other interests, especially since she had such, well, fixed views.

The Major Tutor pursed her lips, tapping a stylishly yellow fingernail on her amber desktop. She began a set-piece mini-lecture on devotion to the profession, on taking every opportunity in a field where such things came seldom these days, on understanding that in such circumstances he could allow no niceties.

Clayton had heard it all before but believed it anyway. He could see the elements of personal advancement in this, but something deeper drove him and the Major Tutor as well: curiosity. Among those souls of true scientists, this was the ultimate addiction which could not be deflected. Both of them wanted to *know*. If minor deception was the price, so be it.

The Major Tutor observed that he would, of course, need special equipment. She could arrange that. But even more important was care, a sense of timing, even downright guile. Clayton understood.

His Major Tutor gave him confidential summaries of Brotherland's construction, or rather, what little was known about it. The utopian colony was the outstanding enigma of the day. What's more, Dr. Rollan had been acquiring advanced technology of an unsettling kind: plasma containment vessels, superstrong magnets, high-quality ceramics and alloys. Could he be building something even stranger than Brotherworld?

These questions the Major Tutor implied with raised eyebrows, and gave him an inventory of recent purchases by the colony. Clayton tucked it away for study at the site.

The task was not without risk. Clayton was an adventurous type, though, determined to get his kicks in life, even if some of them were in the face. He left his Major Tutor firmly resolved.

He accepted Sylvia's invitation, and changed his major subject to Undeclared, in case she should be of suspicious mind. Indeed, some of his friends did mention to him, as he was packing, that Sylvia had casually inquired into Clayton's doings. They took it as sign of female caution; courtship was a rite given much thought in this era, and the preliminaries were often the most rewarding aspect. They slapped him on the back, made nudge-nudge wink-wink jokes, and gave unsolicited and rather explicit advice.

Clayton took the precaution of leaving behind any reading cylinder which could give away his interests. Instead, he took microtexts on social responsibility, even one which denounced the anarchist-cum-free capitalist asteroid communities from which he came. He halfway agreed with the book, anyway. The 'roid clans were rude, unsubtle, even loutish, compared with the fine manners and delicate social distinctions commonly found in California. The books had a point.

2.

They took a standard commercial fusion liner from Earth to Ceres, the conjunction being good. It made the trip under boost at full grav and arrived in five days. There they changed to a slingship. Its electromagnetic accelerating rings squashed them at three gravs for aching tendon-stretching moments, then abruptly set them free on a long arc across the solar system, out to the motes of asteroids. The ship moved like a darting wisp among the stately slow sway of worlds.

Their target was a lonely, rolling hunk of iron called Hellbent. The other people on the slingship were rough, silent types, ill-kempt and grimy, with little hope of ever getting far enough ahead to afford a true, full-water bath, or food not force-grown, or clothes of something finer than the fibrous weaves they wore.

All Hellbent men and women sucked a lean milk from bare, spongy rock. Economics had decreed Hellbent's smelted products valuable for one booming generation, and had then snatched away its blessings, leaving only a shadowy clan who had too much invested to leave the place. The large docking cylinders and electromagnetic accelerators were leftovers of the glory days, patched up now as the buttress of the economy. Clayton and Sylvia found the maze of sheet-metal corridors forbidding and chilly. The sheen of bare phosphors made them squint.

As they waited near the air lock for her father's shuttle, Sylvia asked, "Did you see that skinny man on the slingship?"

"Uh, yes."

"He was an astrophysicist, I'm sure of it."

"Why?"

"The way he looked at us. He knows who I am."

"Maybe he just thought you were good-looking."

She shrugged this off, impervious to compliments. "*And* his fingernails were clean."

Clayton hid a grin. "A sure sign."

He signed, and felt an itchy sensation as he breathed in. Hellbent was so poor they ran their public rooms at zero humidity. In their hour-long wait the system could extract a gram or two of vapor from their breath and sweat, an involuntary tax of fluids.

Clayton's home was never *this* badly off. He felt a twinge of guilt at thinking of his parents, laboring in the chilly grit of a rockworld not greatly different from this. He should visit them, but the cost was prohibitive. Sylvia had paid all the expenses this trip; he could never have afforded it. One of Clayton's classmates had even suggested that as long as he was out this far, he might as well nip over and look in at home, too—all this said with an oblivious groundhog smile, never thinking that Clayton's parents were on the other side of the solar system from here. To Earthsiders, like New Yorkers of the centuries before, everything beyond their neighborhood was a single, amorphous Elsewhere.

The shuttle arrived with a clanging thump. When the thrumming pumps had stilled, the two of them floated into the bare, gloomy loading bay. A silvery body nestled there, sleek and chromed. From its nose a powerful beam of ruddy light turned and regarded them like a malignant eye out of the coagulated night. As they glided forward, Clayton saw it was a shapely fusion flitter, gleaming with polish. The slim craft was studded with portals that winked and sparkled as he passed, looking exactly like enormous green and yellow jewels. Its nose was subtly asymmetric and spindly guidance rods studded its sides, deftly functional. It was a work of art.

Two men, dressed in Spartan simplicity, stood inside the welcoming ramp. Clayton saw instantly that they were Brothers, the famous product of Dr. Leon Rollan's cloning experiment. And indeed, he could not tell one Brother from the other.

"Welcome to the Gates of Paradise," one said, giving Clayton a warm handshake.

"I'm uh, pleased to enter," Clayton replied.

The Brothers greeted Sylvia even more warmly, as was fitting. Clayton glanced back and saw a small clutch of Hellbent's miners, muttering to each other and staring with frank, wide-eyed awe at the magnificence of the shuttle. The well-lit interior had upholstery of woven silk and linen. Here and there were plump pillows of subtly stated opulence. The bulkheads were a deep ebony, adorned with crescents of glittering ruby-like stones and iridescent splashes of some blue-white jewels. It all represented the firmament itself, artfully arranged to lead the eye from one glowing high point to another.

"Incredible!" Clayton cried out.

"Oh, this is the old one," Sylvia said.

"There are others?" Clayton could not take his eyes off the rich fabrics.

"Oh yes." Something flickered in her eyes and he guessed that she saw a sudden contradiction springing up. She believed in selfless politics, yet had grown up among wealth such as this. Perhaps she was a classic TwenCen liberal, able to hold such a contradiction in a mind that chose to see only that it desired.

"So much…" he hinted delicately.

"We have to keep up appearances, or my father's economic position in the macro-economic community will suffer."

"Oh, yes, quite reasonable. People do pass judgment, don't they?" It felt lame, somehow, but her sunny smile banished his frown.

An alabaster dome topped the passenger lounge, a miniature copy of the famous mosque in Cairo he had seen the year before—except even more glorious, here, in a sun-defying white.

"Of course." Sylvia gestured lazily at the Hellbent miners, who now crowded around the foot of the ramp. "It's for them, really. They like to see how well a truly different system works."

Soon they were boosting at a steady 1.5 gravs, the ship humming with solid assurance through slick blackness. Clayton could tell immediately from several constellations, and the orange disk of Jupiter aft, that they were arcing above the ecliptic. Hellbent was merely the nearest 'roid to Dr. Rollan's famous experiment. Hellbent chanced at this moment to be close to the point where Brotherland intersected the ecliptic plane every eighteen months in its oblique path. Lonely miners perceived Brotherland as a glittering, sparkling speck high up in the darkness, orbiting serenely above the affairs of ordinary men.

Clayton saw it within a few hours. The Brothers kept to their business, scarcely sparing more than a few phrases after their warm greeting. They spoke to each other in a strange argot, which Clayton could not penetrate, so he turned to staring dreamily out the faceted portals. These were unusual in design, not giving a clear vision at all, but rather a series of refracted images, as though peering through a jewel. Certainly the sculpt-engineer had gone to a great deal of trouble to create the effect. The multiple perspectives complimented the design of the walls, but Clayton found it hard on the eyes.

Through this layered set of images Clayton first saw the glowing eye of the Vortex. It was burnt-gold near the center, brimming with crisp light. Around it was a halo of red, and then an encircling, smolderingly blue haze. He strained to see the very center and was rewarded with a tiny, virulent twinkling. At first he could not be sure it was not an optical trick of the odd portal. The dot flickered like a will 'o the wisp in a distant, churning fog. Clayton felt his breath quicken, a tingle of excitement. The dab of light hardened. He was sure now. The dazzling white speck was the roiling glow emitted by matter as it cried out in its incandescent agony, flaring brightly for one long groaning instant before it plunged forever down the yawning Schwarzschild throat of a black hole.

3.

A massive star at the endpoint of burning has a central temperature of ten billion degrees and is nearly a billion times more dense than iron. Unable to burn any longer, its core collapses, the nuclei there break apart, and implosion begins. There is a "bounce" and the implosion turns into the classic supernova explosion. Matter initially near the stellar core rapidly expands and cools. Often the core left behind forms a neutron star or a black hole. These bizarre end products of stellar death throes were the principal focus of much of TwenCen astronomy.
—Supernova Debris (2nd edition)
Valerie Thompson, 20078

The glory of Dr. Rollan's artful empire unfolded in concentric rings: the Vortex. Its fuzzy, glowering blue rim was a disk of dust that slowly spiraled inward, toward its death. As dust swarmed ever-nearer the hole, friction among the particles heated them. Stirred by magnetic fields to a turbulent frenzy, they radiated. Farthest out, a blue oxygen line dominated the emission, giving this rim the color of a week-old bruise. Farther in, the faster-circling gas sputtered with an angry red. Radiation stole angular momentum from the dust. This minutely affected the orbiting particles, lowering them slowly inward.

Clayton quickly calculated in his head. It would take years for a dollop of dust to bleed inward, into the next band, a brimming mustard circle. Then the compressed dust flowed into the sunlike, white-hot hub where a fraction of its rest mass energy was released, fully thirty percent. There lived the black hole, the dynamo that made this work.

"You can't see it," Sylvia said helpfully. "It's only a speck, anyway, no bigger than your fingernail."

"Uh, amazing." He must not appear to know very much.

"See the collectors?"

A wide array of photon collectors orbited above and below the luminous disk. Sylvia said, "They provide the energy we sell to the inter-planet runs."

Clayton watched the filmy sheets turn in their own elliptical orbits, feasting on the light that burst from the rim of the black hole. They were hundreds of kilometers away, but the scene was lit with dazzling intensity. The collectors beamed microwaves across the solar system, he knew, providing in-flight power to ships. That cut transport costs enormously. Rollan had been the first to provide the service.

"I don't follow the details, but it *is* lovely, isn't it?" Sylvia said with little-girl wonder.

Clayton agreed, but yawned and languidly said, "Uh huh." He shouldn't seem too interested and would make some sketches as soon as he was alone.

He allowed himself one more moment of rapt appreciation. The Vortex glowed with the mere waste energy of vast forces at work. The disks turned, huge economic flywheels steadily rendering ordinary asteroid debris into limitless wealth.

"There's home!" Sylvia cried.

Until now the banks of dust above and below them had hidden the jewel of the system.

Further out, beyond the blue band, all was a mottled darkness, blotting out the stars behind. Further still, the infalling dust thinned. Beyond this shroud, Clayton could see the true marvel, the Hoop.

It was a thin glowing strip, as ripely blue-green as Earth on a summer's day. The inner rim of the Hoop was lit by the glow of the Vortex, its light funneled out and focused on the Hoop by the scalloped plates of the dust. This conserved most of the radiance and delivered it to the Hoop, bringing warm temperatures to its delicately contrived biosphere.

Clayton knew from sketchy information available through the UCLA library that a monolayer shield floated on top of the Hoop's atmosphere. He could see the sheen of Vortex-light scattered by that thin air-trapping film, high above a cottonball cluster of cirrus. Below, basking in radiance, were shimmering lakes and softly undulating hills. At the "equator," the inward curve of the Hoop, a long lake stretched, dividing the span.

Sylvia said excitedly, "Have you ever seen anything so beautiful?"

"Never," he said with complete conviction.

"The forests, the green hills..." Sylvia peered dreamily at the swelling Hoop. "Our Eden..."

Clayton realized she meant the "natural" beauty of the Hoop; he had thought she meant the marvelous engineering that made the thin slice of biosphere possible. He suppressed a disbelieving smile.

They slid outward toward the Hoop. He guessed the entire Hoop was a few kilometers thick, and they were only perhaps twenty kilometers from the black hole itself. Yet the tiny sucking mote provided brimming light for an entire ecology.

The hills swept by, revolving cool and serene, as he watched. The Hoop circled the Vortex every seven minutes, a giant bicycle tire without spokes. But perspectives were awry here. The irreality of a glowering, gnawing mass-eater so near to placid forests was too jarring. He shook his head, dazed.

A faint pattering came through the alabaster dome of the improbable ship.

"Ah!" one of the Brothers said. He hastily dipped the nose down toward the Hoop.

"What was that?" Clayton said, alarmed. Any accident so near the virulent maw—

"A small error," Sylvia said calmly. "We probably hit a cloud of dust that strayed from its course, is all." She smiled with the confidence of a person for whom the technical problems were always someone else's. Clayton had noted that she was becoming more easy-going, less severe, as they voyaged out from Earth's bright confusions

Once told, he understood. The infalling dust was supposed to be channeled down in a parabola, flowing above and below the Hoop by a wide, safe margin. Some errant matter had brushed them.

They descended rapidly. As they dropped toward the slowly gyrating Hoop, the Brother pilots warbled to each other in their strange, insular tongue. The ship looped outward and passed over the nightlike outer side of the Hoop, where ice rimmed the terminator. The Hoop eclipsed the Vortex and darkness descended. Beneath the sole luminescence of the distant speck of the Sun the ice was blue.

"My father says this is where the past ends," Sylvia said, her face pensive and distant.

He reminded himself that to her this spectacular vista was as homey as a back yard. yet he could see that homesickness welling up in the expectant pout of her mouth. Her high cheekbones gave her a severe, imperial look; the mouth belied that now. She was a woman of profoundly felt currents, emotions that at UCLA had found expression in ideas. Now her depths emerged. Her contradictions only made her more alluringly mysterious to him.

"And this—" Clayton had not yet digested the spectacle of the Vortex "—is the future?"

"Why, of course." To her the intricate waltz of light and matter, wheeling here in infinite black, was the family farm, a fact of nature.

He had thought of her as a kinswoman of sorts, reared in a place more like his 'roid origins than the comfortable plush of Earth. But this place, despite his preparation, was bizarre to him. He began to understand how different she was, and felt the tug of a sublime strangeness. He remembered his Major Tutor's calculating eyes and a confusion of motives swirled in him for a moment. Only the grandeur of the spectacle outside made him put all thoughts aside.

They came over the rim of the Hoop, clouds allowing brief glimpses through to the verdant fields. From the Vortex a wedge of light poured outward, trapped between the blankets of infalling matter. The twin sheets of dust resembled plates that necked in to intersect at the hot central spark. As they converged the plates glowed, giving the bands of blue and yellow and brilliant white that he had seen earlier.

They arced around the face of the Hoop, toward the permanent high noon of the equator. The monolayer sheen was turquoise here, with distorted cumulus clouds wedged against its restraining boundary by the rising heat from below.

There—a lessening. The entrance hole, a swiftly-forming leak in the system which allowed ships in and out. It would be open for mere moments.

They turned and glided through it, thrusters focused down now. Here the jockeying was difficult. The ship into through the hole, through thick cloud layers, and emerged suddenly above a careening landscape. The Brothers worked furiously now, vectoring sidewise and up, and now down and aft, as they matched velocities and accelerations in an intricate gavotte, descending toward their landing field.

The ship, so graceful in vacuum, now seemed to have the aerodynamic properties of a brick. Clayton shrank into this couch, dizzy.

What would seem a simple problem in vector mechanics back at UCLA became a sickening whirl. He felt the eternal power of matter over abstractions. This was nothing like piloting among serenely orbiting asteroids.

Thumps, rattles, a hollow *whoosh*. Landfall.

The side of the ship furled up. Clayton followed Sylvia down the ramp into the lush valley. A golden haze hung idly over the vast sweep of lawns, azure lakes and artfully arranged forests. Above, the Hoop curved away in both directions, arching up into a blue fog. In the middle distance groves of oak studded the tawny hills, reminding him of California. Further away, rough masses of pine swathed the rumpled land in a grip of dark blue-green.

"It's…lovely," he said.

Three deer emerged from a grove of elms nearby, never giving them a glance, and meandered into a wooded gully. A falcon wobbled on changing air currents high overhead, then began a descending gyre. Above all this hung the incessant Technicolor blaze of the Vortex.

"Hail!" came a voice nearby.

Clayton turned to see a ruddy-faced man who seemed about sixty walking stiffly toward them. The famous Dr. Ludwig Rollan showed his years, yet his eyes vibrated with resolve beneath the golden glow of the haze.

The next moments' customary greetings went by Clayton without leaving any lasting impression, for he was fascinated by Rollan's presence. It is common to be so overwhelmed by the celebrity of the great that at first the actual person seems unreal, too compact and mortal to have been the source of such renown. Clayton had never met anyone of remotely the stature or mystery of this tanned, fuzzy-bearded man who shook his hand slowly, blue eyes self-assured and calm and questioning. He could think of absolutely nothing worth saying. His mind hung in a vacuum, spinning fruitlessly as Sylvia hugged and kissed her father and peppered the grizzled, indulgent man with questions. They exchanged affectionate jokes.

Then Dr. Rollan said, as if prompting Clayton, "I gather you are a young man deeply committed to our ideas here."

"Sure am," Clayton said, without specifying which ideas he meant. This place was certainly ripe enough with demonstrated ideas, with practical applications of huge forces.

"Fine!" Dr. Rollan slapped Clayton on the back with gusto. "Out here we used to get lots of the other kind, you know, good Clayton."

Clayton nodded, supposing that Rollan meant the grimy, no-nonsense inhabitants of the asteroids, perhaps begging for handouts. They were interrupted by Rollan's dog, a mongrel who seemed to become immediately fond of Clayton's leg. On Earth dogs were rare, other than as a delicacy, and Clayton did not know how to respond. The dog was ardently embracing his knee. Rollan was distracted, pointing out the sights, so Clayton gave the dog a quick, experimental kick. It backed away.

Dr. Rollan took them to a handsome dinner in a vast, green stone country house, termed the Hostel. "Just something the Brothers made up as a greeting," he said, ushering them into a vast communal dining hall. "Do you know what this is?" he asked Clayton.

"Well, uh, a cafeteria," Clayton said uncertainly.

"No!" Dr. Rollan cried good-naturedly. "It is our equivalent of church."

They stood watching the throng for a moment, and soon Clayton saw what he meant. The Brothers dined with a ritual seriousness, passing food and observing social graces with a deadpan earnestness. Evidently the sharing of food was a crucial observance to them.

Clayton found it unnerving—a huge long room, filled with Brothers, and Sisters who looked exactly like each other. Dr. Rollan had cloned them all from the cells of a great genius of the last century, a social philosopher who had updated Marx and mixmastered in a blend of oriental religion, self-help, and moral philosophy. The high steepled wall above bore the statement.

A WEED IS MERELY A PLANT SOMEONE DOESN'T LIKE.

Clayton frowned, trying to figure out the implications. Rollan's dog reappeared, this time eyeing Clayton's leg avidly but keeping a respectful distance. He glowered; it cowered. Fascism evidently worked with dogs, Clayton deduced.

"The Brothers and Sisters, they're really all alike?" he asked, to be saying something.

"Exactly," Dr. Rollan said.

"Nothing's *perfectly* copied every time," Clayton said.

Dr. Rollan answered crisply, "Circus knife-throwers know it is possible to be perfect, and one had better be in *anything* truly earnest."

"Yes sir?" a Brother answered at the Doctor's elbow.

"Oh, I didn't mean you, Ernest. Meet Clayton."

Ernest was a burly version of the others, obviously the product of an extensive exercise program. He wore his shirt open to the navel, where a mat of brown hair exuded a husky scent. Clear blue eyes regarded Clayton closely. There were three women behind him blank-faced, obviously waiting until his attention returned to them.

"Glad to shake the hand of anybody can give the Missy a good time," Ernest said, pinching Clayton's hand in a viselike handshake.

"The...the Miss?"

"Miss Sylvia," Ernest explained. "She's the untouchable around here."

"Ernest means I don't take part in their sexual calisthenics," Sylvia explained lightly.

"Not genetically allowed, you see, good Clayton," the Doctor said. "Would pollute the strain."

"Ah." Clayton liked something in Ernest's direct, gruff manner and was pleased when they sat at a table together. The all called Dr. Rollan the Handyman as though he were some mere technical assistant. Clayton thought this odd, and even stranger that Dr. Rollan beamed at the nickname. There were greetings all around, but then the Brothers and Sisters fell into rapt conversation with each other, leaving the three genetically different people to themselves.

Food arrived, succulent and steaming. All vegetarian, of course. It was passed on plates of a hard, black, heavy substance which Clayton guessed must be a product of the Vortex itself, matter transmuted by the intense heat of the inner accretion disk.

Ernest quickly downed several glasses of sweet, smacking his lips and pronouncing in detail its qualities. "Try more, good Clayton," Ernest said, slopping some on the table as he refilled Clayton's glass.

"Uh, thanks." He wished everyone wouldn't use the "good" preface, though he noted others routinely using it. It reminded him of old ideas about conditional training. Ernest began telling stories about the farming and labor of the Hoop, dominating the table talk for a while. They were seldom quick and light, and each had a point delivered with the leaden quality of pig irony.

Clayton got on well enough with Doctor Rollan, discussing his parents' asteroid community and the ever-changing economics of the Belt. The Doctor had once been a rockhound himself and still remembered much of what a catch-as-catch-can existence it was. At first the venerable man merely nodded and grunted assent, but as Clayton described his father's company and their hardships, Rollan began to break in with stories of his own, snippets of information, good-old-days counter-examples. Slowly, listening respectfully, Clayton knitted together a picture of the man, filling in the space that had remained obscure in the biographies he had read.

4.

Rollan had found the Vortex entirely by accident.

He was born Norman Vladimir Rollan, son of good New Socialist parents in middle Europe. At that time the planners were attempting to arrest the long economic slide of his native land, and so sent teams into the newly opened asteroids. Their National Mission was to return raw materials for smelting in high orbit.

Rollan was fully committed to the ideals of his government, and volunteered for prospecting duty. This was a chancy affair, involving long low-energy orbits between likely asteroids. Exploratory robots, however intelligent, had failed; they had no intuitive feel for the crannies which concealed lucrative metal deposits.

The North Americans had gotten to the obvious candidate 'roids long before, so the European prospectors were forced to explore lesser targets—those with odd spectra, or hard-to-reach orbits out of the ecliptic plane.

Rollan was not a lucky prospector. He turned up countless examples of the most common 'roid—a spongy assemblage of boring elements, with no seams of rare metals. He failed to find even one carbon-rich rock, which would at least have paid his expenses.

He was on his final run, having boosted up to three km/sec at an angle of thirty-seven degrees out of the ecliptic plane, fatalistically pursuing a lumbering mountain of unpromising rock. He never reached it. Fifteen hours after his pulsed launch in a cramped, one-man slingship, Rollan registered a flash of x-rays that looked like the preliminary burst from a solar flare. Normally the warning system would give him an hour to find a 'roid and hide behind it, out of the sleet of protons spewing from the sun.

But when Rollan swiveled his 'scope around to confirm, the sun was an ordinary disk. Turning, he found that the radiation came from a spot high above the ecliptic. Unless he had ventured off on this oblique orbit, he would not have been within range to pick it up.

He tracked the spiky, slow-simmering x-rays for hours. They came from a pinprick of UV emission which was swooping down toward the asteroid belt.

Rollan expended his remaining reserve fuel and met the firefly dab of yellow. As he approached he expected it to swell into a 'roid profile. Instead, he nearly collided with it, believing it must be still a long distance away. Only his acceleration meters warned him. seconds before it was too late, of a sudden steepening of the local gravitational potential.

It was a black hole, the first ever found in the solar system—still grinding up and devouring the small rock it had intersected, yielding the burst of x-rays.

Rollan was a competent astrophysicist and he knew a fortune when he saw one. Observation of distant quasars had shown that their dazzling energies came from matters processed by vast black holes at a galactic center. Matter cast into a disk around a black hole could yield an entire menu of radiation, exotic materials and useful high-energy particles.

He also knew the hole was dangerous. His Earthside training had included elementary magnetic fusion methods;

this qualified him to fly a solo slingship craft and make his own repairs. That came in handy.

He fashioned a magnetic trap for the hole, keeping a respectful distance. The hole, despite containing the mass of a medium-sized asteroid was only a millionth of a centimeter wide. Rollan's magnetic bottle could be strong but crude.

Slowly, gingerly, he towed it back to a grubby 'roid station, where he kept silent about the contents.

Only when he reached the tinny magnificence of Ceres Station did he begin to use the hole, injecting ordinary dust and extracting energy by driving magnetohydrodynamic generators. Electrical power was still at a premium and he—or rather, his National Mission—prospered.

The hole was kept a secret, but even its profitability did not stave off the effects of a general economic recession. Rollan's National Mission folded up. Most of his countrymen went home, but Rollan managed to keep the hole—he had never revealed, even to his superiors, what fed the generators.

These hard times were the crucible which hardened and shaped Rollan. The decline of the New Socialist nations—democratic or totalitarian, first world or tropical, strict or reformist—led him to believe that only a wholly fresh kind of society could bring about the aims of the old utopian thinkers. With the hole he began a series of brilliant economic coups, manufacturing exotic materials and plasmas for anyone who could pay. He brought his own asteroid and moved it to a concealing orbit at a steep tilt to the ecliptic. This isolated him from the Belt society, allowing time to refine ore as he refined his own ideas.

He hired trusted assistants, all ideologically pure. He went on frequent, high-boost journeys to Earth, carrying his wares, and returned with huge credit balances payable in the banks of the Belt. He was an early investor in the self-replicating robot companies, buying over a third of them in the first decade of the industry.

Then came the long plateau of his life. He traveled little and worked ever-harder. Inevitably, news of the hole escaped.

Eager, ferret-eyed scientists came to inspect. The nations of Earth attempted to confiscate it. The Belt laid claim to "mineral rights." The system-wide economic community demanded that it be classified as a natural resource, the "proper heritage of all mankind."

In a sense, it was. Astronomers had long believed that the solar system began with a nearby supernova explosion. It had occurred in a star of about ten times our sun's mass, blowing outward a huge expanding shell of debris. A sector of this outrushing, highly radioactive junk collided with a neighboring dust cloud, compressing it.

Once begun, gravitational contraction proceeds apace. within a thousand years the jolt applied by the supernova made the dust cloud shrink into a sputtering, newborn star, with an attendant disk which would eventually form planets.

All this could be deduced from the unusual concentrations of rare elements in present-day meteorites. The radioactive elements of the original supernova had long since decayed into daughter and granddaughter elements, a telltale signature of a violent birth for the solar system.

What had *not* been anticipated, though, was the fate of the original supernova remnant. A black hole formed, from matter crushed inward while most of the dying star rushed outward. The hole was of relatively unimportant mass, scarcely more than a mountain's. It was swept along in the chaos and currents of the explosion, and eventually formed part of the collapsing cloud that made the solar system. It apparently reached the imploding dust cloud late in the formation, and took up an orbit not fully aligned with the ecliptic. This gave astronomers a fix on the original rotation axis of the supernova star, and helped formulate detailed numerical studies of the titanic event which had given birth, eventually, to all humanity.

Rollan didn't give a damn. He regarded astrophysics as a mildly interesting but fundamentally useless activity, unless it could be used to extract further wealth from the hole. After giving the scientists minimal time to study the hole—now surrounded by a complex system of infalling asteroid dust, transmutation cylinders and furiously working robots— he closed the entire community to outside visitors.

Earth had long maneuvered to gain control of the hole. Rollan favored neither Earth not the asteroids, on grounds that it was silly to select one bull over another on the basis of the beauty of its horns, when what mattered was that you lived in a china shop.

He maneuvered the 'roid belt interests into successfully countering Earth. In return they asked for preference in patents derived from the hole. Rollan freely gave that, demonstrating again his balancing act between the two economic giants. However, patent rights were all he would grant. All else was cloaked in isolation.

Scientists came to inspect and were turned away. Observations from afar were neatly blocked by the huge clouds of asteroid matter that Rollan sent orbiting in toward the hole, masking whatever enormous engineering feats were going on. Specialists hired for the tasks were sworn to secrecy. Their memories were wiped clean when they left Rollan's employ.

As the years stretched on, no scientists ever managed to wangle an invitation to see Rollan. He evaded government surveys of his holdings, keeping all but a few workers at a great remove from the actual hole site. Rumors circulated that his self-replicating machines were roving the high-azimuth orbits above and below the belt, searching for raw materials not claimed, or even other black holes.

The happy years of progress and expansion were punctuated by Rollan's marriage to a woman of the Lunar Nirvana Colony. The Nirvanites' short-lived experiments in "human-animal genetically altered communality" had led to public outrage. There were some interesting, unanticipated side effects, however. The breakup of Luna Nirvana greatly enhanced the market in collies and cougars who could take care of the children and run the house, too. It created a whole new industry in big game hunting, promising more nearly even odds.

But the experience left Rollan's wife a shattered vessel, a docile receptacle for his idealistic impulses. Sylvia was their only child. Inspired by his vision, Rollan thereafter devoted himself to the cloning program necessary for the new society he envisioned.

5.

Generally ignored in twentieth century astrophysics was a hard problem—what happens to the bulk of the mass ejected from a supernova? Does it all turn to mere drifting interstellar dust, as many supposed?

The explosion occurs in the "carbon flash," when the carbon nuclei begin to collide and fuse. The energy released by carbon-burning heats the core without letting it expand, vastly increasing pressure. This means carbon-level nuclei can remain bonded into a solid form even as they are ejected in the explosion.
—Supernova Debris

Morning. As Clayton awoke he saw drowsily that multicolored streamers of light lanced across his room, rippling the far wall with elegant traceries of shifting blues, greens and oranges. This resonated with his Technicolor headache, a momento of the sweet wine from the night before. He groped from the bed.

Through curiously thick windows he saw the great planes of the accretion disk, a broad stripe that ran straight across the sky. A pale eggshell blue stretched away into oblivion, merging with the fuzzy vision of the Hoop itself, arcing up and away. The spectacle turned dry equations into exotic flourishes of almost kinesthetic delight. He longed to see better, to be able to pick out the robot shepherds who tended the accretion disk. They would be mere dots against this magnificence, lost in the glare, but they could tell him much from their location and movements. His heart pounded.

He tapped the window. It gave back a solid *thunk*. He felt its slick surface, marveling at the density and thickness of the glass. Each pane was faceted at its edges, refracting splashes of light. Even for a man of Rollan's expansive style, it seemed an incredible indulgence.

"Good morning, sir," a voice said behind him. He turned. It was Ernest, the man from dinner yesterday.

"Are you ready for your bath, sir?" Ernest asked, holding out a towel.

"Well, sure." He hadn't expected such service. And Ernest's respectful "sir" he liked better than "good Clayton." Ernest was so devoted to Sylvia that Clayton automatically took him for a rival. It was reassuring that the man apparently knew his place.

Clayton began to shed his pajamas, but Ernest knelt before him and undid the buttons, saying "Allow me." As the man slid the pajama bottoms off, he observed Clayton's state on tumescence (caused by the vision of the accretion disk, plus a full bladder) and offered to provide any sexual service required.

"Uh, well, no, ah—no, not my kind of thing," Clayton gasped.

"You're sure?"

"No!"

"Perhaps one of the Sisters, then? I can summon Pauline or Hadley quickly, they are nearby."

"No, no, nothing thanks."

Ernest nodded gravely and then smiled. "Anything you want, that's what you'll get. Our ideal is selfless service here, sir."

"So I see," Clayton muttered.

"Hot rosewater and vanilla soap?"

"What?"

"Followed by a plasma ionizer rinse," Ernest suggested. "Stimulates the body, while quieting the mind." He nodded significantly at the still-horizontal member.

"Yes," agreed Clayton, smiling inanely, "as you please."

The bath was reached by a slick slide down from his room. The swift journey surprised him, even with Ernest's warning. He plunged into a communal bath, an opulent bowl which was unpopulated save for himself.

Ernest stood at the edge and asked solicitously, "Music? 3D?"

He selected a melody that featured flutes, their notes dripping like a waterfall. Through the translucent walls he saw a moving shadow and abruptly realized that he was surrounded by an immense aquarium. Huge fish, clearly the off-shoots of the old Lunar Nirvan experiments, swam in amber light, gliding without curiosity up to the walls and peering at him. They mouthed something but he could not make it out. A poem, perhaps. The fish had been good at that, were frequently published. He wondered what they ate.

He had only a few minutes before breakfast to draw sketches of the Vortex and Hoop, from memory. At the ample meal they were surrounded by the hubbub of the communal dining room. Brothers and Sisters everywhere brought forth and devoured huge glittering plates of eggs, toast, cereal, ham. Following Uniformism beliefs, the ham was a vegetarian substitute, but Dr. Rollan assured them that it tasted remarkably like true pig flesh. Systematically they ate and left. Clayton could not keep track of the streams of bodies or follow their odd accents.

"They all seem to be about, uh…" Clayton began.

"Twenty-five, on the nose," Dr. Rollan said. "They all came out of the cooker at exactly sixteen when I started the experiment, nine years ago."

"They're all sort of older brothers and sisters to me," Sylvia said. Clayton noticed she had forsaken her constant Earthside garb of severe pants and blue cotton work shirt. Now she wore a little white gown which came to just below her knees. He liked especially the wreath of marigolds clasped with slender blue slices of stone in her hair.

"All the same genotype," Clayton said. "And you hold the patent?"

"I have published the 'specs," Dr. Rollan said. "Anyone can clone more Brothers and Sisters if he or she likes."

"They *are* handsome," Clayton said politely. Actually, he was already tiring of them.

"A simple formula, really," Dr. Rollan said. "I hired the best DNA artists to make me a chain with no inherited diseases, yes. That much is commonplace. But fashioning the right personality mix and making it breed true in the conception tubes—that was no trifling matter."

"I see," Clayton said. "To get the right sort of worker for—"

"No no!" Dr. Rollan was agitated. He stopped slicing the blue-brown fake ham and frowned furiously. "The exact personality type does not matter. I know my ideas are not widely known in the reactionary citadels of Earth—and of course they are roundly despised among the 'roid rabble—but you must have gotten some misinformation somewhere."

"I just—"

"The point is that those societies contain a contra*dic*tion, a dialectical one, it you will. Earth, with its billions of citizens, preaches the virtue of tolerance, of passivity, of conformity. But who does it reward? The heads that poke up above the crowd! It is impossible to free them of their adulation of the special unless it becomes impossible to *be* special!"

"That's a scientific fact," Sylvia put in. "Father gave Brotherland its own dialect, too—it's the easiest way to program their worldview."

"Ah."

"You are training to be a social scientist, Mr. Donner," Dr. Rollan went on, cutting his cube of ham precisely into smaller brown cubes, all alike. "You must realize the central problem! One cannot carry out reproducible experiments on human societies. They are not a controlled environment."

"Well, yes."

"So I constructed this world, to prove that Uniformism will work. Here we can illustrate the central tenets of progressive thinking, begin the true evolution of Post-Socialist man."

"Through controlled experiments."

"Yes. We will demonstrate that Uniformism produces more material goods, higher pleasures, healthier bodies."

"And you'll drive the 'roids into a depression, by out-competing them."

Dr. Rollan chuckled. "It is *they* who preach the virtue of their vaunted free markets."

"But my father's operation—"

Dr. Rollan smiled shrewdly, his eyes rolling upward in amusement. "Free markets…can be costly."

When he returned to his room, Clayton quickly finished unpacking. He assembled the telescope which he had dismantled and hidden among his belongings. It was stubby and could not give fine resolution, but it did not need to. Its heart was a spectrum analyzer which attached like a lamprey to the base.

Clayton pointed the telescope at the huge strip of light that hung like a ribbon wrapping the sky. He would have liked to do this outdoors, but there he would have been quickly spotted. He sighted the telescope through the thick windows and thumbed the instrument into action.

Rollan's ingenious design of the inflowing matter made astrophysical observation of the black hole impossible from a great distance. The infalling matter masked the hole except for the thin wedge in the equatorial plane—which was blocked by the Hoop itself.

Clayton focused the telescope on each of the Technicolored bands of the accretion disk in turn. The spectrum analyzer recorded emission lines, buzzing and humming to itself.

There was a wealth of information here and Clayton began to perspire slightly, his heart thumping. He punched in commands for a finer scan and then heard the door behind him opening.

"Clayton!"

He jumped. It was Sylvia.

"I, uh, I'm—"

"You *must* come to see the harvesting. The entire quadrant is there!"

He stood speechless for a moment before realizing that Sylvia could not see the telescope behind him. "Well, sure, just give me a minute, huh?"

"Just one!" she cried happily, and left.

He quickly stripped the telescope into its components and hid them.

As a Festival of Commonality it left Clayton feeling curiously left out. The Brothers and sisters harvested their wheat, all right, using lightweight machinery and considerable skill. But they chattered together in the indistinguishable patois that was beginning to irritate Clayton.

They all referred to Clayton as "sir" on the few occasions when they addressed him. Clayton felt rather swell about this until Sylvia mentioned that to be exalted above the commonality was in fact a denigration, so "sir" was a term of polite contempt. Ernest had used it, he recalled, in very nearly every sentence since this morning. Had the man become surly over Clayton's romance with Sylvia? Or from Clayton's rejection of his advances? Clayton studied Ernest's brooding face, but could read nothing. Though Ernest looked like all the other Brothers, a certain musky confidence hung about the man, though unescorted by very much apparent cleverness. He decided the man was either very deep or very shallow, and as with many people, it was difficult to tell which.

Dr. Rollan tried to labor with them, sweating profusely, stripped to the waist. The man was old, of course, even neglecting the times he had spent in the coldsleep vaults while his self-reproducing machines had built the Hoop. He so earnestly wanted to be included among the Brothers and Sisters that he ran the risk of overtiring himself. Indeed, he quickly became ashen-faced and had to sit down. Clayton had to admire the chaste and consistent selflessness in the man.

"See how...well they...work together," Dr. Rollan observed while he shakily took a drink at the water trough.

Clayton agreed. He and Sylvia watched from the side of the fields, since he, as an outsider, was not allowed to take any part in the joy of production. Sylvia was in rapture. She confided to Clayton that she loved everything in nature, except perhaps anchovies.

Dr. Rollan said meditatively, gesturing at the laboring lines, "They are the future, young man. Superior to the mess humanity has made of itself."

Like most idealists, Dr. Rollan loved mankind in principle and disliked it in very nearly every particular. "Do you plan to spread the Brotherhood and Sisterhood?" Clayton asked mildly.

"Where?" Dr. Rollan seemed genuinely puzzled.

"Perhaps to those new worlds discovered around Tau Ceti?"

"Good lord," the old man said crankily, "I wouldn't *run away* from the problems of the human race. We have to face them here."

Clayton nodded, but frowned.

That night Clayton could not sleep. The vegetarian diet had proved an ineffective cushion for the weight of wine that had landed on it. Still, he was too cautious to go wandering about on his own. Best not to arouse suspicions.

He sat up reading, and quickly grew tired of reviewing the old text, *Supernova Debris*. It was the last major work on the subject. Dr. Rollan had denied scientists access to the black hole and to Brotherland, so astrophysics had gained little from his discovery. *Supernova Debris* contained many speculations which could not be verified.

He put it aside and turned to an old text on social theory, tracking down details of the halt-remembered Model of Utopias, a classic treatise created by the nearly unreadable but famous social theorist and nudist, Darko Drovneb. Brotherland seemed to have all the characteristics. The textbook discussion rang uncannily true.

The Brothers and Sisters made a point of communal values, keeping their culture pure and without diversity. Rollan's program of genetic uniformity helped that, and also aimed at the second Drovneb characteristic: no change with time. Experiments required unchanging conditions, after all. Even more important, change implied that something had been wrong before.

Drovneb's third signature—a nostalgic and technophobic atmosphere—fit, too. The Hoop was a giant farm, recalling Earth of centuries ago. And the Brothers and Sisters knew little or nothing of machines beyond their farming equipment. Robots and Dr. Rollan made the Hoop work, with nearly everything technical kept above the bottled atmosphere. On the Hoop, all was simplicity.

And Rollan himself provided the fourth characteristic—an authority figure. He insisted on being called the Handyman, but it was clear that his word was law. He had built the very ground they stood on, after all.

Only in the final Drovneb characteristic was there some doubt. *Social regulation through guilt*, the book said. *Responsibility is exalted as the standard of behavior.*

Clayton frowned. The Brothers and sisters seemed remarkably guilt-free, compared with the constricted folk of Earth. Maybe the rural surroundings simply made them seem more easy-going.

Certainly their absurdly low-tech agricultural methods were politically imposed, hopelessly inefficient. Yet apparently it worked well enough to make a profit for Brotherland. Of that the Handyman was proud. He kept the fields of the

Hoop as a nostalgic echo of the farms of centuries ago, and it seemed to work. The ghost of Rousseau walked here.

He wearily thumbed off the book. The Drovneb parameters fit nearly every utopian society of the last five centuries. The theory predicted a common end—as soon as the authority figure died, things began to slowly unwind. Diversity, curiosity, simple human orneryness—all conspired to bring down the golden pillars of dreams.

He wondered what would happen when Dr. Rollan was gone. Could this pinwheel in the sky roll on?

He sighed and fell into an uneasy sleep.

6.

Someone was following them.

At first Clayton thought he was projecting his own free-floating anxiety about being discovered, but after a while the signs became unmistakable.

Dr. Rollan had proposed that Clayton and Sylvia hike around the Hoop. There were striking vistas and pleasant forests in a world which was only five kilometers wide but over a hundred kilometers long.

While they were crossing a monotonous checkerboard of cultivated fields Clayton first caught sight of a distant figure far behind. There were so few Brothers and Sisters working alone, a single person was noticeable. The Hoop rose up into the sky, distorting perspective. The distant person seemed above them, looking down from a blue-green carpet that curved away into misty cloud. As Clayton watched, the figure disappeared behind a tree. Later, he glimpsed a flicker of movement as they mounted a hill.

Always at the same distance. Always the quick ducking out of sight.

A polite way for Rollan to be sure his daughter didn't get into trouble? Or to keep tabs on Clayton?

They explored the long equatorial chain of lakes which divided the Hoop into two shores. A leisurely walk around the Hoop took about a week in the half-g centrifugal gravity. It was several days before he could adjust to the sensation of journeying only a few kilometers and finding a wholly new environment. Tropical pineapple fields gave away to Alpine forests, which yielded to fertile river-valley vegetable farms, all managed by dutiful Brothers and Sisters. Overhead, occasional flying robots adjusted the humidity, shifted the clouds, tinted the air with mixers and catalysts, like angels over Eden.

They hiked through crisp rolling hills, wholesome flatland wheat and cloying dense jungle. Sylvia seemed to bloom with every kilometer of progress. One day they avoided the 'roidrock communal home of the Brothers and Sisters, and instead camped in a dense knot of oak trees. Their canopy blotted out the Vortex, bringing a false night.

Sylvia luxuriated on a bed of moss, which Clayton had gathered at her request from the moist upper limbs of the trees. "Moss is a parasite, after all," she had said. "It uses trees; *we'll* use *it*."

Clayton toasted compressed tofu bars over yellow flames. "*This* is home," Sylvia said languorously. She sat on a large stump (careful thinning was necessary for a balanced biosphere) and said, "*Real* nature."

"Um," he agreed.

"Where people can be people again." Her dress fluttered like a white sail in a breeze, a craft promising far destinations. Oak leaves stirred above in the firelight, making moving shadows as does the wind on the sea.

"Right."

He took her some tofu, hot and jacketed in a crisp black crust from being held too long in the flames. He collapsed to his knees before her as she bit into the creamy warm taste inside. She smiled in lazy acceptance and he kissed her. He drew in his breath deeply, feeling himself on the verge of a great abyss. She parted the dress and shrugged free of it. The fabric fell like a table cloth on the broad stump, herself as the meal. He was tired of trying to be underspoken and witty. He inhaled and a musky scent of her swarmed into him. Insects chirruped in the twilight. "Ah," she said. The filmy dress, the thick air—if he had been sensible, he would have worried about his heart. She smiled, silkily stroked his neck, and slid the backs of her knees over his shoulders.

As they hiked the next day, the Technicolor ribbon overhead rippled and flexed, like a living flag. Clayton watched it as closely as he could, a hand lifted against the glare. He could see now and then a chunk of asteroid debris escorted in by robots. The tidbit then slowly wound its way through the outer edge of the accretion disk. From this equatorial angle he could see much that was unknown about the disk—the coal-dark lanes of thickening dust, the sudden yellow flares of magnetic reconnection further in. When alone, he took notes and used the finger-sized camera tucked snugly into his belt.

Rollan still imported earth technology when it seemed in accord with the aims of Brotherland. Clayton had respectfully brought up the subject of contact with Earth. Rollan had visited there several times, making mysterious business arrangements, brushing aside questions from scientists. "Why go to Earth at all?" Clayton had asked. Rollan had rolled his eyes and replied, "Why do people go to zoos?" and would say no more.

They had nearly circumnavigated the Hoop when Clayton saw a craft many kilometers up in the air. That seemed impossible, and indeed it was—there were no clouds at that moment, and he was staring straight through the cap on the atmosphere, into space. As he peered upward the silvery craft glided across the eggshell-blue bowl and dropped below the hills to his right.

Sylvia was becoming tired, so he left her to swim in one of the shallow, sparkling lakes. They were partway through a jungle zone and he found the going rough as he hiked the kilometer upward, into the hills.

He had never thought about precisely how the Hoop atmosphere was held in, so the shortening of the jungle trees came as a surprise. Here and there, dotting the thick tangle of vines, were great mango trees, their fruit purplish red or vivid yellow among the massive leaves. Among them loomed rubber trees, each with a tap to catch its milky sap, cool columns stretching up into air thick with moisture.

They were all cut at the top. And as he struggled upward amid green, cloying vegetation, he saw why. The monolayer which capped the atmosphere curved down to the ground nearby.

Their trunks sheathed in vines, the trees were stately among screaming cockatoos and pigeons which boomed through the leaves on whirring wings. He saw that the Brothers and Sisters must have kept the trees trimmed at the top to avoid their puncturing the thin, shimmering layer of flue that arced down out of a clear sky and came to earth not much further up in the hills. Clayton struggled on.

Abruptly he came to a steep drop—or so it felt. The trees stopped and he was looking straight down to ice. In a dwindling perspective he saw the silvery craft slow and fire mooring lines into a great cliff of sea-blue ice, scarcely more than a hundred meters away.

He nodded to himself. The Hoop's rotation gave a centrifugal gravity pressing outward, which was "down" on the Vortex-facing face. On the night side the effect was reversed, making it useless. Why would a ship land there, among the ice which Rollan used as backup fluid storage?

A cargo bay irised open in the ship's side. Robots edged something bulky from the bay. They towed it across to the ridged ice, which to Clayton's perspective curved down and away. He squinted as the robots and their cargo drifted into shadow.

Their chunky load looked like ice, too.

But why bring ice here, where there was plenty already?

And where did they get it?

He leaned forward to see better. His foot twisted on a last root that clung to the edge of the soil. He pitched forward, arms windmilling.

A large hand grabbed his shoulder, hauled him back.

Panting, he turned to see who it was. Ernest said, "Dangerous up here, sir."

"Uh, yes."

"Sightseeing is fine but you have to watch yourself."

"Yes, I didn't expect—"

"Not good to leave the Miss alone like that, either."

"Well, no, but—"

"You're supposed to enjoy yourself, sir."

"Well, I was merely looking—"

"Don't concern yourself with those machines," Ernest said solemnly. "They're different from us."

Flustered, Clayton wondered what the man could possibly mean. "Yes," he said, "they have more arms."

"Huh?" Ernest's heavy brow wrinkled in puzzlement.

"Forget it."

"Thing is, like the Handyman says, you got to stick to the good and true."

"What?"

"The fine way the light from the Vortex plays on the pebbles in a brook. Hard and true."

"Oh." The man seemed a cretin.

"Bright and clear."

Clayton nodded, though Ernest seemed neither of those things.

"You shouldn't be up here," Ernest said stolidly. Then, as an afterthought, he added, "Sir."

7.

It had been Ernest following them all the time, of course. Once revealed, he stuck like glue, taking none of Clayton's broader and broader hints.

They stopped for the "night"—really just a scheduled time when the windows were firmly covered against the steady Vortex glow—at a Hostel. As usual, the Brothers and Sisters were polite, generous and totally uninterested in their visitors. Clayton got a haircut from them, at Sylvia's request. Ernest, whose muscles rippled beneath a tight T-shirt, attracted his usual covey of Sisters. Some were quite graphic in their intentions for recreation after the dinner hour, stoking him as they passed and cooing voluptuously. He grinned and accepted this as his due without making much of it. Clayton became uncomfortable at these continual erotic interruptions of their dinner conversation. There was also an embarrassing moment in the restroom. He had gotten used to the fact that there were no separate facilities for Brothers and Sisters, but was still surprised when Ernest offered to compare the lengths of their members while they stood near each other at the urinals. From Ernest's laconic remarks, Clayton gathered that Ernest felt the winner would have proved something.

Rummaging for something to say, Clayton bitingly remarked, "You can't compare flowers until they're fully grown."

Too late, he realized that Ernest might easily take this as a frank invitation. He fled without even pausing to zip up.

Back at the log communal dinner tables, Clayton deliberately kept Ernest's glass filled with the sweet, red wine all the Brothers and Sisters drank. It was undistinguished, but it loosened Ernest's tongue.

"Sure, we ship the good grain to the 'roid people. Good trade," Ernest said.

"Profitable?"

"Pays expenses."

"Do you work on the engine repair for those tugs, the ones that haul the grain?"

Ernest nodded. "Don't like it much."

"Why?"

"Me, I like the simple work."

"Growing food?"

"Right. We've all got to rotate jobs, though."

"Why?"

"You know—prevent elites from forming." Ernest pronounced "aye-letes," his brow furrowed at the thought.

"I've noticed you don't use much farm machinery."

"Work's not so good if you got to use machines all the time."

"You all agree on that? Even the ones who're doing the hoeing and plowing?"

Ernest Looked irritated. "Why should any Brother or Sister think different?"

"Well, on Earth there's a different opinion every ten feet you go."

"That's Earth's problem."

Sylvia nodded. Clayton did not wish to get into an argument with her, so he probed in a different direction. "Do you work on other kinds of propulsion engines?"

Ernest sat very still. "Like what?"

"Well, fusion drives, that sort of thing."

Ernest looked confused. His small eyes darted around the room, but the long rows of Brothers and Sisters were babbling to each other with rapt attention. "Why would I do that?"

"Well, to carry cargoes further around the solar system."

Ernest became more agitated, simultaneously trying not to show it. The man obviously had no grace under pressure. "I don't think about those things," he said lamely.

Clayton didn't believe Ernest thought about much at all, but a few moments later in the conversation he let drop the term "ramscoop" and Ernest visibly started. *Ah.*

By this time a Sister was tugging Ernest away for what promised to be only the first bout of the night. Sylvia explained demurely that the Brothers and Sisters—who referred to themselves as the People—were agreed that the Hoop should be filled to the limit with more People. "The greatest good to the greatest number," she said. "That's the rule, isn't it?"

He could hardly disagree, especially since it promised to keep the already drink-sodden Ernest well occupied throughout the "night."

Two hours after Sylvia fell asleep in their small monk-like cubicle, Clayton rolled soundlessly from bed. He made his way through the cool ceramic hallways of the Hostel, easily dodging the small staff that went about necessary chores. The Hoop's advantage in having a constant source of Vortex-light, and thus a relentless growing cycle for crops, was somewhat offset by the inconvenience of tending to the fields even at "night." Still, Rollan's prescriptions for social unity decreed that a vestige of Earthside ritual be maintained, not least because it gave a rhythm and unity to the communal experience. So the Hoop ran on the standard 24-hour day, with few workers staying up through the nominal night.

Clayton slipped away from the Hostel on the side away from the central fields, since he was bound for the edge. No one followed.

He reached the Hoop's rim quickly. He had tucked into his rucksack for the circumnavigation a small infrared telescope. By standing on the very edge of the Hoop, he gained the greatest angle of observation, and thus could see furthest into the accretion disk near the black hole. Puffing from his run, he settled into the roots of a towering elm tree and steadied the telescope on his knee. He was near the edge of a cliff. The monolayer buried itself into a rock ledge only meters away. Beyond that began the blue ice. He wondered momentarily about the curious incident of the day before, and why robots would deliver ice to an already ice-heavy outer face of the Hoop. It seemed innocuous, but Rollan's obsessive secrecy throughout the construction of his clockwork world naturally made Clayton suspicious.

He shrugged and set to work.

More than ten kilometers away, straight up the sky, blankets of dust curved in toward the glowing disk. Clayton strained to pick up detail in the murky cloak. It blotted out the stars, but against the infalling, circling sweep there hung glittering ivory motes. Robots, shepherding the ground-down 'roid dust. They looped gracefully among the shrouded dark lanes, probing and pushing with electromagnetic snow-plow fields.

The telescope translated infrared into visible, and gave a smoldering complexion to the slowly churning dance above. High out on the Hoop's axis, robot trawlers swarmed like ant beetles around an asteroid. They picked it apart like insects dismantling unlucky prey. They crunched it into the dust which spiraled inward, toward—

Something glimmered at the edge of perception. He had idly swept the 'scope by the accretion disk, knowing that the virulent glare there would soon blind the instrument. But somehow the glowing region near the black hole was lit by mere twilight flares. He peered at it by looking away, using the edge of his vision. Yes, the luminous core was dimming. But the brilliance of the disk to both sides did not ebb. Then, just as he was sure he was not making a mistake, the momentary darkening waned. He had the impression that a mask was being drawn away, both physically and metaphorically. For only a few seconds, something had blocked the light from the innermost disk.

Something in orbit. Something big.

He calculated rapidly. If it was that close to the black hole, its orbital period—

He finished just as the dimming came again. A few seconds of twilight, then the returning brilliance.

Something about a kilometer in diameter was orbiting the black hole, about two kilometers from the hole itself.

Far enough outside the furnace heat of the infalling disk to keep it intact. But close enough in that no one would think to look for it. The glare of the inner disk blinded all but the most sophisticated instruments…and Rollan had made quite sure that no scientist with such equipment ever got near the Vortex.

Clayton nodded to himself. A perfect hiding place.

Or nearly perfect. After all, he had found it.

But what was it?

The ramscoop, certainly. His Major Tutor had supplied Clayton with enough information from around the solar system—invoices for machined parts, electromagnetic webs, pulsed power systems, superconducting magnets—to arouse ample suspicion.

The authorities had let Rollan's pin-wheeling utopia go spinning along its benign orbit for decades, as long as they were sure it was an essentially harmless experiment. Virtuous, even. After all, Rollan did supply grain and other food to the 'roid communities. And his microwave net did transmit power at marketable rates to ships on fast boost between the planets.

But the accumulating evidence of the invoices suggested that Rollan was far more ambitious than he seemed. Rollan had built a ramscoop engine. With it he could launch cargoes into interstellar space, colonize other solar systems. This was illegal, indeed, immoral. Humanity had not yet agreed on a strategy for interstellar exploration. If Rollan sends a ship carrying the mere cellular ingredients for Brothers and sister, he would be able to colonize whole worlds with the seamless sameness of the People.

That could not be allowed. Obviously.

Clayton shook his head and muttered a string of unoriginal but satisfying obscenities.

He had thought he would craftily reap a harvest of interesting astrophysics, and return to UCLA in triumph. Now his worst fears were confirmed. He would have to find out more about the ramscoop.

Crack.

He jerked to alertness. The snap of a breaking limb echoed through the stillness of the elm grove. Birds stirred and fluttered above. Clayton listened and thought he could hear the rustle of someone slowly prowling through a glade nearby.

He saw a flicker of movement. It was one person, following a remorseless rectangular pattern. Searching.

He crouched down and crawled away from the edge of the Hoop, careful not to disturb the rich piles of leaves slowly turning into loam. They would crackle and give him away, and anyway, the act would probably upset some ecological equation somewhere.

He wished that this "night" was real, could provide sheltering darkness. It occurred to him that the perpetual day banished the entire Earthly freight of associations planetary spin gave humans: darkness, gloom, evil, uncertainty, general bad news. Brotherland was a place where day reigned eternal, illuminating all with piercing light, permitting no obscuring dark. Even the shadows were Technicolored mimics of the Vortex bands.

He wished fervently for a touch of darkness now.

Clayton moved cautiously, senses alert. Everything looked different from this angle. No wonder, he mused, that little children were hard to understand. Their world was dominated by anthills and tree roots, lakes of mud and mountains of garbage, chair legs and dog bellies, pant cuffs and big-toed feet, the musty mystery up mummy's dress. Who wouldn't be cranky?

A figure moved among distant trees. Clayton considered making a run for it and then realized that, after all, he hadn't really done anything. Just looked over the edge a bit, natural tourist curiosity.

Still, he didn't like being followed. He worked his way around an outcropping of rock, his soft-soled shoes making no sound. There was a rustling in the trees just below him. Clayton crouched. Only a meters away a man emerged, scanning the path with a careful eye. Ernest.

Without thinking, Clayton picked up a hefty rock and tapped the big man on the skull.

Ernest dropped like a felled ox. Clayton froze, horrified at his own act.

He had committed the first act of violence in a perfect world.

Ernest came to as Clayton staggered toward the Hostel. He had hauled the bulky man two kilometers in an over-the-shoulder carry and felt like a laboratory rat on an endless treadmill.

"Hey…whatcha…hey," Ernest muttered.

Clayton dumped him and told his rehearsed story, about finding Ernest where a small landslide had caught him.

"Yeah?" Ernest rolled up his eyes as if in thought.

"Uh, yeah."

"Well, man's got to get hit, head wound's the best."

"Oh?"

"Quick."

"Oh."

8.

The return of Clayton and Sylvia to the Central Hostel, where Dr. Rollan ruled, was cause for festivity.

Even Dr. Rollan's dog was glad to see them, yelping and leaping at Sylvia. The dog eyed Clayton's leg adoringly but kept a respectful distance, eyes glinting with what Clayton took to be the *Fueherprinzip*.

Dr. Rollan beamed, laughed, celebrated—the perfect host. He even commented warmly on Clayton's hair, mentioning that it now resembled the Brother style, simple and utilitarian.

"Glad to see it, good Clayton," Rollan said.

Clayton chose not to remark that he had gone along with Sylvia's haircut proposal primarily because of the pleasant effect she had anticipated that the soft, short brush would have on her upper thighs. Instead, he had more of the aromatic wine.

That evening, as part of the sporadic celebration, Dr. Rollan instructed the worker robots who tended the Vortex to perform for Clayton and Sylvia. In they came, hundreds of the ivory motes streaming out from the glossy bands. Further

54

legions descended from the banks of infalling dust, leaving only a skeleton crew of robots to keep the dark shroud on its slow sure gyre.

They flitted gnat-like through a momentarily opened hole in the monolayer. At Rollan's wrist control, the puncture spread. It was a suddenly swelling black circle, into which the robots swooped. Then it zipped shut, summoned together again by intricate molecular commands.

The robots extended silvery wings and swarmed through the Hoop's upper atmosphere. They formed letters, symbols, pictures. Against the sky the metal fleets swooped, performed adroit feats, defied gravity. Clayton realized there was no gravity up there. Centripetal force held him pinned to the Hoop, but only the mild brush of the air acted on the flying robots. He craned his aching neck to follow their darting arabesques.

As they set to work on a large cloud. Clayton stole away. The crowd went *ooh* and *aahhh* as the cloud purpled, swirled reformed. The robots were crafting some momentary sculpture from it. An ear poked out. An eye appeared, winked. Then a full, round lip.

"Oh, it's Daddy!" he heard Sylvia cry as he slipped inside the Hostel. The Handyman made some self-deprecating reply.

Clayton quickly found what he was looking for. Rollan's private quarters were encrusted with command and control modules, detailed sequencing arrays, luminous graphics—the nerve center which controlled Brotherland and the Vortex. He felt like a spy, slipping through the doorway. Myriad columns and rows of data rolled on opalescent screens. If he could encipher even some of this, the right scrap of information—

"Why—*Clay*ton!"

He jerked his attention away from the hypnotic welter. Sylvia stood in the doorway, eyes round with shock.

"I, uh…"

"What are you *do*ing?"

"Ah, I just wanted a look around the place."

"Daddy *never* lets anyone in here."

"Why not?"

"*You* know."

"The family secrets, right."

She said archly, "I'm sure you really do understand. You're just being difficult."

He wondered how much she knew? She was quite smart, but one could be blind toward those one loved. He sighed. "Come on, let's go see the rest of the show."

"It's nearly over. Robots bore me, really." She looked at him from the corner of her eyes, a lightly enticing smile curving her cool lips. "Besides…wouldn't you really rather go to our room?"

Her invitation was irresistible, her buoyancy contagious. Her dress fluttered in a vagrant breeze, as though she herself had just returned from a short, graceful, effortless flight in the uplifting air. Clayton sighed and gave himself over to her, though he knew he would have to try something daring if he was ever to make any real progress.

9.

As the supernova expansion continues, the shell will fragment into clumps whose size is difficult to predict. Despite turbulence and magnetic disruption effects, some clumps should survive. They should have densities in the range of their initial formation. Rapid radioactive decay will leave many of them in states of virtually pure silicon, magnesium, or carbon. Indeed, carbon chunks will be most common, probably in the form of graphite. However, if at the onset of expansion the incipient lattice structure were face-centered cubic, this form could persist. Numerical simulations of this stage are costly and unreliable, so it appears unlikely that theoretical work on this topic can proceed further without some observational spur. Since such solid supernova debris is not luminous, attempts to observe it near supernova remnants in the galaxy seem doomed. This are of research thus appears to be at a dead end.

—Supernova Debris
Valerie Thompson, 2078

Later, he tugged her along the passageway, nervously watching the doors ahead.

She whispered, "But honestly, I don't see why we have to—"

"Shhhh!"

They walked softly through the rest of the Hostel, avoiding the distant sounds of movement as the skeleton night shift went about domestic duties. Sylvia led him through an obscure side exit and they stepped into glaring daylight.

She began sleepily, "I still don't see—"

"I want a better look at the Vortex robots," he said. "And I'm pretty sure your father wouldn't let me."

"Did you *ask* him?"

"What you don't ask for, they can't deny you," he said nimbly.

"But he might get angry if—"

"Where did you say they usually landed?" If they stood here and talked it all out, eventually somebody would come by.

"Over there, beyond that hill. The maintenance station is buried under that grove of apple trees." She pointed reluctantly.

They skirted around the Hostel and made their way, keeping well back in the leafy shadows. A section of hillside slid aside at Sylvia's command; he was quite sure the voice-actuator would have rejected him, perhaps set off a jangling alarm. He had gently gotten information from her after a sweaty tussle in bed. She had drifted into sleep, but a plan bloomed in his imagination.

After their graceful aero demonstration, some of the Vortex robots had stayed on the Hoop, for routine repairs. Sylvia walked through the quick, darting teams of shiny robots without giving them more than a glance, assured that they would get out of the way. They did, too. Awake now, she was quite willing to show off more of her father's vast empire, though it became obvious that she knew very little about how any of this worked.

In the back row he saw a bulging cylindrical thing perched on a launch platform. Atop it was a transparent bubble. A giveaway; automatic machines don't need observation domes.

"Can I take a look inside that one?" he asked casually.

"Um, I suppose so."

She was alert yet quite willing to go along with his curiosity. The point, she had reminded him regularly, was to free people from machines, so that they could think primarily of each other again. She repeated this as they climbed up the rungs of the large, pear-shaped vessel. A hatch hissed open. Inside, she tapped a command phosphor and a voice obediently asked, "Yes, Missy?"

"We'd like some drinks."

"Of course. I have fresh squeezings of fruit, pure water, sniffer ale—"

Clayton was no longer listening. His eyes swept the control panel, understanding its elegant simplicity immediately. His hands flitted over an actuation pad and the boards lit up. He tapped in a command. Standard stuff; his 'roid experience paid off.

The drinks were already splashing into opulent crystal glasses. The disembodied voice interrupted its offerings of food with, "Oh, sorry, I shall have to belay catering while we are under acceleration."

Sylvia blinked. "Acceleration?"

"Yes. Please be seated."

Clayton felt a gentle throbbing under his feet, then a tug, "What—ow!" Sylvia cried, as she tumbled onto a divan which had sprouted from a bulkhead.

"We're taking his personnel robot for a ride," Clayton said. "To see the sights."

Sylvia's eyes widened. "You, you…"

"Quite."

The craft rose with obedient, smooth competence. The hillside rolled away and they sprouted from it, a thin tongue of orange fire licking at the tail. Clouds wreathed them, visible through the transparent dome above. The ship asked, "Destination?"

"The Vortex," Clayton said.

Sylvia could have rescinded his order at any moment, he knew, but something strange had come into her eyes. She stared at him, a prettily puzzled frown marring her forehead. He had taken a move without consulting her; perhaps she was so surprised by this unique event that the possibility of a serious outcome to this adventure had not yet occurred to her? Somehow her crisp intelligence, so apparent at UCLA, was submerged. The true Sylvia seemed ever more unfathomable. She sat on the divan, stroking its gold lamé upholstery with a slow distracted rhythm.

Clayton had worried about the monolayer, but he needn't have. It parted as they rose, unzipping a slice of raw black sky. The ship poked through it and free.

Sylvia said, "You don't mean to—"

"Oh, but I do," He smiled.

They sped swiftly toward the brimming disk of light. Dust thumped and rasped and sang against the hull.

"You'll tell me when the x-ray of UV count gets high?" Clayton asked the ship.

"Of course, sir. Bit I shall rotate my body away from the disk itself, so as to absorb the radiations before they reach you."

"Good idea."

"I was designed to think of such things."

"For what mission?"

"To take Dr. Rollan on his journeys to the Vortex"

"To study what?"

"That I do not know."

"Does he go often?"

"Sadly, no. He has seldom made the trip this last decade."

"Any idea why?"

"No sir," the ship said stiffly, and Clayton wondered if its programming used "sir" as Ernest did.

"Clayton, I want to go back," Sylvia said. He recognized the petulant vixen approach—pouting lip, whinny singsong. But somehow he knew she did not mean it.

"No. I want a look at this."

"My father will be angry—*very* angry."

Ah, threats. "I think he'll understand. He was like me, once. Come on. Your father had curiosity."

"He was thrown into a place and a time, by impersonal historical forces," she said, as if she had memorized it from somewhere.

"Is that from one of your father's speeches to the Brothers and Sisters?"

She looked surprised. "Well, yes."

"There's another similarity."

"What?"

"He was an astrophysicist, once."

She looked blank. "You're not, you're—" Then a furious look crept over her face.

"Right. I'm majoring in astrophysics."

Sylvia gritted her teeth and swore bitterly, her words like spat tacks. He said nothing.

She began to shout at the ship, commanding it to turn back. When there was no answer she pounded on the firm but padded walls.

"It's no use," he said mildly. "I've switched the ship to control panel operation only."

"How—why—"

"I'll explain later. Don't think badly of me simply because I did what I had to do. Just…give me time. And watch."

He knew there was little time before Dr. Rollan would be after them, and less still before the ship would reach the inner edge of the accretion disk. His heart thumped as he swung into the observation chair. It was mounted on gymbals and shafts, allowing easy movement about the transparent dome. Filtered telescopes and array sensors hung nearby, available at a gesture. Astrophysical luxury.

The central riddle of Brotherland came riding toward them, trailing clouds of glory.

They were coming down now, falling at an angle toward the accretion disk. It turned like an immense Technicolor phonograph record. Luminous bands shaded from blue to orange to red and finally, at the furiously spinning inner edge, a startling glorious white. Clayton felt a giddy, seasick sway as the ship matched orbital velocities with the disk. Each striated section was at a different temperature and gave off its own speckled, roiling glow. He could see flecks of still-solid stone being swallowed at the outer rim, then ground into fuel by friction's raw rub.

But toward the center, where the burning fire was a searing point, he caught a flicker of movement. Something solid, something large...

Sylvia was talking to him, using reasonable tones of persuasion, softly undulant. To Clayton it was babble, lost in the background pops and rumbles that echoed through the ship. Tidal stresses from the hole? He could not follow her quixotic changes any more. He concentrated on the shadowy thing ahead.

He punched in directives and the ship smoothly shifted, pressing them into their couches as it set off in pursuit of the inky thing that—Clayton saw clearly now—as orbiting at the edge of the disk, but not *in* the disk.

"It's in orbit around the hole, perpendicular to the disk," he said wonderingly.

"*What* is?" Sylvia asked sharply, but even she was puzzled, frowning up at the strangely somber, gleaming thing.

The distorting sweep of light made it hard to be sure. "It's no ramscoop vessel, at least," Clayton muttered to himself. So those suspicions, at least, had been wrong...

The surface of the thing caught the disklight and threw it back in a shower of minute glimmerings, a thousand thousand wavering ice-blue candles buried deep in the slumbering mass.

Extract sample, Clayton ordered the ship.

A small flitter launched itself across the foreground, braked, then buried itself deeply in the target.

The bulk's slow rotation brought into view long, webbed tubes mounted on the surface.

"Accelerators," Clayton said. "That's what your father bought the electromagnetic guns for."

"What?"

"To adjust the orbit of this big mass. To make up for the friction it encounters when it punches through the disk. And people Earthside thought he was building a starship..." He smiled mirthlessly.

Sylvia peppered him with questions, but he brushed them aside. They watched silently as a sample-fetching robot returned and thumped into the lock. In a moment the ship's flawless servants had conveyed the sample case up to the receiving bay. Clayton snapped it open.

Into his hand floated a brilliant, icy stone.

"I don't..." Sylvia touched the cold, hard thing.

"It's a diamond."

"What! Are you...sure?"

"It fits with some studying I've been doing. Supernova debris is mostly rubble, junk, hydrogen gas. But the compressed star could form solid matter. At those temperatures..."

"Solid carbon? That's what diamond is, like graphite, isn't it? Only harder."

"Yes—far more compressed. The supernova star did that. The center imploded into a black hole, the outer layers blew away—and somewhere in the middle, *this*."

He looked wonderingly out at the slowly spinning mass. It had lumps and hummocks, like any other small asteroid. Yet each minute turn brought forth myriad fresh facets of hard, cool blue, of russet, of sulfurous yellow.

"But who would ever have thought...always considered molecules, maybe a few pebbles at most. *This*...a chunk so big..."

He estimated distance, angle. He tried to think of something on a human scale to compare it to, something as worthy of this rich relic from a time beyond the first dim stirrings of earthly life, beyond the first raindrop, beyond the blind dumb buttings that formed the sun itself.

He whispered, "It's one whole stone. A diamond as big as the Ritz."

"The what?"

"A hotel in Boston. A fabulous hotel."

She said sardonically, yet distantly, "For the rich only, I'll bet."

"For the different."

"Sure they're different. They have more money."

Clayton could not argue of such infinitesimal things, could not take his eyes from the blissfully turning body, host of a billion starlike blue-white promises.

10.

"**G**ood Clayton!"

The rasp of Dr. Rollan's voice on the radio yanked him from his reverie.

"Daddy! Look what we've *found*," Sylvia cried gladly.

Clayton put out a hand to block the small TV camera she swiveled, to transmit the image before them. Sylvia veered it away from him, and focused on the vast stone.

"Think of it!" she said. "It must have drifted in here from those dust clouds the robots are always working on, bringing in from the Belt. Dummies! They didn't recognize what it was."

Clayton began carefully, "Sylvia, you should wait and—"

"No, don't you understand? If Clayton—I know he's impetuous, Daddy, and I have to admit it, a liar, too!—If Clayton hadn't stolen this ship and come out here on a jaunt, we would never have known this was here. It would fallen into the hole!"

Clayton said, "It's moving exactly perpendicular to the disk. That minimizes the friction it feels when it passes through the plane of the disk. Anyway, it's far out, at the edge of the disk. A small, steady push could keep it in this orbit for a long time."

"That's quite right," Dr. Rollan's voice came crisply through the panel speaker. "This object will no doubt prove very interesting to study. Meanwhile, I must insist that you return at once to the Hoop and leave—"

"No, Daddy! I want to *explore*. A diamond this big, it's—why, I wonder if when you stand on the surface, you can see yourself, little pictures of yourself, waving back? All the way down to the center!"

"Sylvia, there is all the time in the world to—"

"Never mind, the charade won't play," Clayton said.

Rollan asked menacingly, "What?"

"A diamond asteroid, orbiting just so precisely that it won't fall into the hole easily? But perfectly positioned so that when it is above or below the plane of the disk, it's screened by the infalling dust? And so that nobody can see it from the Hoop? The only way I suspected it, was through its eclipsing. There was a quick little flicker as its shadow passing between me and the disk."

Rollan frowned. "I never could figure how to get rid of that."

Sylvia said, "The robots put it there, I bet. They probably were wondering what it was. But with all they had to do, preparing for their air show and all, there probably hasn't been time—"

Clayton laughed, though he sensed this was not wise. "And it just happens to arrive now?"

Sylvia said irritably, "You're making a lot out of—"

"No, he is right, Sylvia," the Handyman said.

"The stone has been here from the beginning. I discovered it at the same time as the hole itself. They were in orbit about each other, even then."

Sylvia blinked. Her mouth opened—first in amazement, then in perplexity, then in a sad, wondrous expression of confused defeat. Finally she shut it, having said nothing.

"Then your biography is wrong?" Clayton asked.

"In part."

"You didn't make your first money out of the hole at all, did you?"

"No."

Sylvia asked wonderingly, "Then, how…"

"He sold chunks of the diamond," Clayton said. "Right?"

"Yes. A little private courier run to Earth, some quiet deals. It was necessary."

Sylvia said distantly, "To finance Brotherland?"

"Yes. I could extract power from the hole, but not enough to buy all I needed. I left the diamond here in the original orbit, where no one would find it."

Clayton added, "We always wondered why you put Brotherland out here. That didn't make astrophysical sense."

Dr. Rollan's voice said wanly, distantly, "Yes…a clue, one I could not avoid."

"But Daddy, why *hide* it?" Sylvia's lips hovered between stunned surprise and quizzical alarm. Yet her eyes studied the huge stone outside with keen intelligence.

"I used chips from it to finance the Hoop."

"But I thought…the black hole…"

Rollan said sadly, "Yes, I could make some profit from energy extraction…but I could see it would not be enough to accomplish…my dreams. Certainly it alone could not support…the economy of the Hoop as it now exists…all the Brothers and Sisters."

Clayton understood everything now. He opened his mouth to speak when suddenly he glimpsed a rapidly growing red dot, high above the diamond asteroid. "What—?"

Ernest's voice boomed through the cabin. "I've come to kick your ass back where it belongs, *sir*. The Handyman, he's taking this pretty hard. I decided to come out here and drag you back, you lying little—"

"Oh, forget that hairy-chested stuff," Sylvia said sharply. "Can't you see you've been outfoxed?"

Clayton found her sudden tart anger endearing. All along he had wondered if she found Ernest's sweaty—well—ear-

nestness somehow attractive. To find that she could so quickly size up the situation, and automatically side with him, gave
Clayton an unexpected jolt of pleasure. He smiled at her and
gestured toward the immense gleaming stone.

"I believe the lady would like to take a walk upon the surface first, Ernest. We'll suit up momentarily. Then I'm sure
I'm quite capable of escorting her safely home, thank you."

The sputtering exasperation that came from the speaker
only deepened his joy.

11.

Clayton took a moment to himself on the veranda. It was pleasant to get outside, away from the hothouse festivities of the Hostel.

Dr. Rollan had declared a holiday. The Brothers and Sisters had set to with an endless round of dances, feats, athletic competitions, songfests and general revelry. Apparently they required no explanation of the holiday, no pretext, but simply gave themselves over to a mad round of heart-warming ritual good spirits. Clayton had never seen people with such capacity, and wondered how such a remarkable ability fit into the dry, acerbic Drovneb parameters. Breathing in the succulent air of ripe fields and sweet promise, he decided that narrow dull Drovneb had missed something vital.

"Are you going to accept?"

Sylvia's sudden question, coming from behind, made him jump. He turned to find her glowing with energy, perspiring from a whirling folk dance that was just now ebbing away in the hall beyond.

"I...I came here to think it over."

"You *have* to."

"Well, I...it's a big decision, Sylvia."

Her mouth formed an incredulous O. "But you could live here for*ever*."

"But I couldn't return to Earth, or even to the asteroids."

"What does that matter? Earth can't compare to *this*, can it?"

He gazed out across the verdant fields, the gentle curve of the Hoop rising up into the sky with a seemingly infinite promise of bountiful natural wealth. There was astrophysics to be done here, yes. Utopian visions, a self-contained universe.

Even if it was founded, finally, on a deception. But still, that false center was a giant jewel, a marvel unequaled anywhere.

"No, it can't."

"Father *needs* you."

"Yes, so he told me when he made the offer." Clayton patted her hand uncomfortably.

Actually, Dr. Rollan had revealed more than Sylvia or anyone else in Brotherland knew. Dr. Rollan's health was declining, an arteriosclerotic gumming combined with gradual, accumulating organ defects beyond the healing powers of man or machine. Rollan was the scientific sorcerer behind the Hoop, and was finding the task more difficult as the great ring spun on. Even minor excitements, such as Rollan's confession to his daughter at the discovery of the diamond mountain, sapped his strength. He needed help.

"You know," he said distantly, "if you hadn't invited me, I wonder how he could have gotten anyone reliable out here."

"You mean any volunteers would have been Earth agents?"

"Well, yes," Clayton admitted uncomfortable.

"Just like you."

"But I'm different, you know that."

"Oh yes, as I know," she said, an enigmatic smile playing on her lips.

Clayton's arrival had seemed an omen to Dr. Rollan, a possible eleventh-hour salvation. Rollan had never trusted outsiders enough to think of bringing them into his gyrating experiment. But now he had to. Sylvia's chance invitation had provided an unexpected opening.

"Is he resting?" he asked to deflect the conversation.

"I checked a short while ago. He's looking better."

"He knows I won't leak information about the diamond."

"Of course," she said mildly. "We trust you."

"Mere knowledge that so many potential diamonds could flood the market—that alone would drive the price to nearly zero."

Sylvia smiled. "Your sacred market system. Too much wealth and it becomes worthless."

Clayton shuffled uncomfortably, rubbed his hands together. There had been so many signs, clues, hints. The thick windows of his bedroom were diamond sheets. The robots he had seen at the edge of the Hoop were bringing a chunk of diamond to store among the ice fields of the Hoop's backside. Ernest's discomfort at discussing technical matters arose from the man's lack of experience at keeping secrets from strangers.

Rollan had not been deeply disturbed by Clayton's discovery. Perhaps the years of keeping the secret had built up a kind of pressure to share it with someone who could understand.

The old man did trust him. Earlier tonight the Handyman—face lined, hands visibly trampling, voice reedy and faltering—had offered to bring Clayton forward as his inheritor, the Fixit Man. To transfer the mantle of humble power.

Rollan's dog came cautiously onto the veranda and sat a respectful meter from Clayton's revered leg. Curiously, the dog acted this way only toward the Handyman and himself, as if all along the animal had sensed some similarity.

"I…I don't know," Clayton said. "I'd have to learn so much astrophysics, how to handle Brotherland, to teach people like Ernest enough to help me out."

"Father can teach," she said laconically.

Clayton nodded. Dr. Rollan knew the quirky ways of the Brothers and Sisters, was sure that he could smooth the way for Clayton. They needed leadership, though of a gentle, self-effacing kind. For in their blissful, nostalgic world, the Brothers and Sisters were unprepared for the inevitable threats the Hoop faced.

One danger was obvious. The mass which was heated and thus lit the Brotherland skies was in turn swallowed by the hole. As the hole's mass grew, its gravitational field clutched the Hoop harder, made it spin faster, stressed the carbo-steel webs that underlay the warm green fields. This would worsen. Only an astrophysicist could solve such a long-term problem.

The handyman had peered at Clayton for a long time this evening, beseeching him wordlessly to shoulder the task. And now Sylvia did, too.

To maintain this idyllic simple communality demanded vast, intricate, gyrating technology, but even that was not enough. At the secret center was not a dark secret but instead a diamond, a luminous cliché of capital.

Something in these contradictions appealed to Clayton's heart.

He took her hand and walked inside, to the railing above the large dance floor. Below swirled the uplifted, perspiring, happy faces.

For the first time tonight, Clayton had begun to sense the strange social cohesion these people felt. They were the Handyman's evermore demanding and uncontrollable hostages to fortune, joyful souls born into a serene world shaped by unseen hands. They spoke to each other constantly, comparing their minor mishaps, accidents, confusions, fretful collisions with reality's unrelenting rub. The tireless torrent of pure, unashamed gossip shared out all misfortunes, tempered egoistic dread, purged anger of its uniqueness. There was a solace in such a thick net of mutually invaded privacies, sexual preferences confessed and exercised under an unblinking sun, angst exposed to the social glare like a skin disease shriveling away beneath searing ultraviolet. Like a height-

a painful *crack* and I felt cold, colder than I ever had been. "What's happening?"

"Your…humans…have a…thing." He was wheezing before each word. "A tool…that…tears…through."

He set me down gently on the cold rock floor. I shuddered out of control, teeth chattering. No air. Lungs full of nothing but pain. The world was going white. I was starting to die but instead of praying or something I just noticed that the hairs in my nose had frozen and were making a crinkly sound when I tried to breathe.

Red was putting on the plastic layers that made up his Mars suit. He picked me up and I cried out in startled pain— the skin on my right forearm and breast and hip had frozen to the rock— and he held me close with three arms while the fourth did something to seal the plastic. Then he held me with all four arms and crooned something reassuring to weird creatures from another planet. He smelled like a mushroom you wouldn't eat, but I could breathe again.

I was bleeding some from the ripped skin and my lungs and throat still didn't want to work, and I was being hugged to death by a nightmarish singing monster, so rather than put up with it all my body just passed out again.

I woke up to my father fighting with Red, with me in between. Red was trying to hold on to me with his small arms while my father was going after him with some sort of pipe, and he was defending himself with the large arms. "No!" I screamed. "Dad! No!"

Of course he couldn't hear anything in the vacuum, but I guess anyone can lip-read the word "no." He stepped back with an expression on his face that I had never seen. Anguish, I suppose, or rage. Well, here was his daughter, naked and bleeding, in the many arms of a gruesome alien, looking way too much like a movie poster from a century ago.

Taka Wu and Mike Silverman were carrying a spalling laser. "Red," I said, "watch out for the guys with the machine."

"I know," he said, "We've seen you use it underground. That's how they tore up the first set of doors. We can't let them use it again."

It was an interesting standoff. Four big aliens in their plastic-wrap suits. My father and mother and nine other humans in Mars suits, armed with tomato stakes and shovels and one laser, the humans looking kind of pissed off and frightened. The Martians probably were, too. A good thing we hadn't brought any guns to this planet.

Red whispered. "Can you make them leave the machine and follow us?"

"I don't know…they're scared." I mouthed "Mother, Dad," and pointed back the way we had come. "Fol-low us," I said with slow exaggeration. Confined as I was, I couldn't make any sweeping gestures, but I jabbed one forefinger back the way we had come.

Dad stepped forward slowly, his hands palm out. Mother started to follow him. Red shifted me around and held out his hand and my father took it, and held his other one out for mother. She took it and we went crabwise through the dark layers of the second airlock. Then the third and the fourth, and we were on the slope overlooking the lake.

The crowd of aliens we'd left behind was still there, perhaps a daunting sight for mother and Dad. But they held on, and the crowd parted to let us through.

I noticed ice was forming on the edge of the lake. Were we going to kill them all?

"Pardon," Red muttered, and held me so hard I couldn't breathe, while he wiggled out of his suit and left it on the ground, then set me down gently.

It was like walking on ice—on *dry* ice—and my breath came out in plumes. But he and I walked together along the blue line paths, followed by my parents, down to the sanctuary of the white room. Green was waiting there with my skinsuit. I gratefully pulled it on and zipped up. "Boots?"

"Boots," she said, and went back the way we'd come.

"Are you all right?" Red asked.

My father had his helmet off. "These things speak English?"

Red sort of shrugged. "And Chinese, in my case. We've been eavesdropping on you since you discovered radio."

My father fainted dead away.

Green produced this thing that looked like a gray cabbage and held it by Dad's face. I had a vague memory of it being used on me, sort of like an oxygen source. He came around in a minute or so.

"Are you actually Martians?" Mother said. "You can't be."

Red nodded in a jerky way. "We are Martians only the same way you are. We live here. But we came from somewhere else."

"Where?" Dad croaked.

"No time for that. You have to talk to your people. We're losing air and heat, and have to repair the door. Then we have to treat your children. Carmen was near death."

Dad got to his knees and stood up, then stooped to pick up his helmet. "You know how to fix it? The laser damage."

"It knows how to repair itself. But it's like a wound in the body. We have to use stitches or glue to close the hole. Then it grows back."

"So you just need for us to not interfere."

"And help, by showing where the damage is."

He started to put his helmet on. "What about Carmen?"

"Yeah. Where's my suit?"

Red faced me. I realized you could tell that by the little black mouth slit. "You're very weak. You should stay here."

"But—"

"No time to argue. Stay here till we return." All of them but Green went bustling through the airlock.

"So," I said to her. "I guess I'm a hostage."

"My English no good," she said. "Parlez-vous Francais?" I said no. "Nihongo hanasu koto ga dekimasu?"

Probably Japanese, or maybe Martian. "No, sorry." I sat down and waited for the air to run out.

10. ZEN FOR MORONS

Green put a kind of black fibrous poultice on the places where my skin had burned off from the icy ground, and the pain stopped immediately. That raised a big question I couldn't ask, having neglected both French and Japanese in school. But help was on its way.

While I was getting dressed after Green had finished her poulticing, another green one showed up.

"Hello," it said. "I was asked here because I know English. Some English."

"I—I'm glad to meet you. I'm Carmen."

"I know. And you want me to say my name. But you couldn't say it yourself. So give me a name."

"Urn. . .Robin Hood?"

"I am Robin Hood, then. I am pleased to meet you."

I couldn't think of any pleasantries, so I dove right in: "How come your medicine works for us? My mother says we're unrelated at the most basic level, DNA."

Am I 'DNA' now? I thought I was Robin Hood."

This was not going to be easy. "No. Yes. You're Robin Hood. Why does your medicine work on humans?"

"I don't understand. Why shouldn't it? It's medicine."

So much for the Enigmatic Superior Aliens theory. "Look. You know what a molecule is?"

"I know the word. Very small. Too small to see." He took his big head in two large-arm hands and wiggled it, the way Red did when he was agitated. "Forgive me. Science is not my....there is no word. I can't know science. I don't think any of us can, really. But especially not me."

I gestured at everything. "Then where did *this* all come from? It didn't just *happen.*"

"That's right. It didn't happen. It's always been this way."

I needed a scientist and they sent me a philosopher. Not too bright, either. "Can you ask her?" I pointed to Green. "How can her medicine work, when we're chemically so different?"

"She's not a 'her.' Sometimes she is, and sometimes she's a 'he.' Right now she's a 'what.'"

"Okay. Would you please ask it?"

They exchanged a long series of wheedly-poot-rasp sounds.

"It's something like this," Robin Hood said. "Curing takes intelligence. With Earth humans, the intelligence comes along with the doctor, or scientists. With us, it's in the medicine." He touched the stuff on my breast, which made me jump. "It knows you are different, and works on you differently. It works on the very smallest level."

"Nanotechnology," I said.

"Maybe smaller than that," he said. "As small as chemistry. Intelligent molecules."

"You do know about nanotechnology?"

"Only from TV and the cube." He spidered over to the bed. "Please sit. You make me nervous, balanced there on two legs."

I obliged him. "This is how different we are, Carmen. You know when nanotechnology was discovered."

"End of the twentieth century sometime."

"There's no such knowledge for us. This medicine has always been. Like the living doors that keep the air in. Like the things that make the air, concentrate the oxygen. Somebody made them, but that was so long ago, it was before history. Before we came to Mars."

"Where *did* you come from? When?"

"We would call it Earth, though it's not your Earth, of course. Really far away, really long ago." He paused. "More than ten thousand ares."

A hundred centuries before the Pyramids. "But that's not long enough ago for Mars to be inhabitable. Mars was Mars a million ares ago."

He made an almost human gesture, all four hands palms up. "It could be much longer. At ten thousand ares, history becomes mystery. Our faraway Earth could be a myth. There aren't any space ships lying around.

"What deepens the mystery is that we could never live on Mars, on the surface, but we *could* live on Earth, your Earth. So why were we brought many light years and left on the wrong planet?"

I thought about what Red had said. "Maybe because we're too dangerous."

"That's a theory. Or it might have been dinosaurs. They looked pretty dangerous."

II. SUFFER THE LITTLE CHILDREN

The damage from the laser was repaired in a few hours, and I was bundled back to the colony to be rayed and poked and prodded and interviewed by doctors and scientists. They couldn't find anything wrong with me, human or alien in origin.

"The treatment they gave you sounds like primitive arm-waving," Dr. Jefferson said. "The fact that they don't know why it works is scary."

"They don't know why *anything* works over there. It sounds like it's all hand-me-down science from thousands of years ago."

He nodded and frowned. "You're the only data point we have. If the disease were less serious, I'd introduce it to the kids one at a time, and monitor their progress. But there's no time."

Rather than try to take a bunch of sick children over there, they invited the aliens to come to us. It was Red and Green, logically, with Robin Hood and an amber one following closely behind. I was outside, waiting for them, and escorted Red through the airlock.

Half the adults in the colony seemed crowded into the changing room for a first look at the aliens. There was a lot of whispered conversation while Red worked his way out of his suit.

"It's hot," he said. "The oxygen makes me dizzy. This is less than Earth, though?"

"Slightly less," Dr. Jefferson said. He was in the front of the crowd. "Like living on a mountain."

"It smells strange. But not bad. I can smell your hydroponics."

"Where are children?" Green said as soon as she was out of the suit. "No time talk." She held out her bag of herbs and chemicals and shook it.

The children had been prepared with the idea that these "Martians" were our friends, and had a way to cure them. There were pictures of them and their cave. But a picture of an eight-legged potato-head monstrosity isn't nearly as distressing as the real thing—especially to a room full of children who are terribly ill with something no one can explain (but which they suspect is Martian in origin). So their reaction when Dr. Jefferson walked in with Dargo Solingen and Green was predictable—screaming and crying and, from the ambulatory ones, escape attempts. Of course the doors were locked, with people like me spying in through the windows, looking in on the chaos.

Everybody loves Dr. Jefferson, and almost everybody is afraid of Dargo Solingen, and eventually the combination worked. Green just quietly stood there like Exhibit A, which helped. It takes a while not to think of giant spiders when you see them walk.

They had talked about the possibility of sedating the children, to make the experience less traumatic, but the only data they had about the treatment was my description, and they were afraid that if the children were too relaxed, they wouldn't cough forcefully enough to expel all the crap. Without sedation, the experience might haunt them for the rest of their lives, but at least they would *have* lives.

They wanted to keep the children isolated, and both adults would have to stay in there for a while after the treatment, to make sure they hadn't caught it, unlikely as that seemed.

So the only thing between the child being treated and the ones who were waiting for it was a sheet suspended from the ceiling, and after the first one, they all had heard what they were in for. It was done in age order, youngest to oldest, and at first there was some undignified running around, grabbing the victims and dragging them behind the sheet, where they volubly did the hair-ball performance.

But the children all seemed to sleep peacefully after the thing was over, which calmed most of the others—if they were like me, they hadn't been sleeping much. Card, one of the oldest, who had to wait the longest, pretended to be un-concerned and sleep before the treatment. I know how brave that was of him; he doesn't handle being sick well. As if I did.

The rest of us were mostly crowded into the mess hall, talking with Red and Robin Hood. The other one asked that we call him Fly in Amber, and said that it was his job to re-member, so he wouldn't be saying much.

Red said that his job, his function, was hard to describe in human terms. He was sort of like a mayor, a local leader or organizer. He also did things that called for a lot of strength.

Robin Hood said he was being modest; for forty ares he had been a respected leader. When their surveillance device showed that I was in danger of dying, they all looked to Red to make the decision and then act on it.

"It was not a hard decision," he said. "Ever since you landed, we knew that a confrontation was inevitable. I took this op-portunity to initiate it, so it would be on our terms. I couldn't know that Carmen would catch this thing, which you call a disease, and bring it back home with her."

"You don't call it a disease?" one of the scientists asked.

"No...I guess in your terms it might be called a 'phase,' a developmental phase. You go from being a young child to being an older child. For us, it's unpleasant but not life-threatening."

"It doesn't make sense," the xenologist Howard Jain said. "It's like a human teenager who has acne, transmitting it to a trout. Or even more extreme than that—the trout at least has DNA."

"And you and the trout have a common ancestor," Robin Hood said. "We have no idea what we might have evolved from."

"Did you get the idea of evolution from us?" he asked.

"No, not as a practical matter. We've been cross-breeding plants for a long time. But Darwinism, yes, from you. From your television programs back in the twentieth century."

"Wait," my father said. "How did you build a television receiver in the first place?"

There was a pause, and then Red spoke: "We didn't. It's always been there."

"What?"

"It's a room full of metal spheres, about as tall as I am. They started making noises in the early twentieth century…"

"Those like me remembered them all," Fly in Amber said, "though they were just noises at first."

"…and we knew the signals were from Earth, because we only got them when Earth was in the sky. Then the spheres started showing pictures in mid-century, which gave us visual clues for decoding human language. Then when the cube was developed, they started displaying in three dimensions."

"How long is 'always'?" Howard Jain asked. "How far back does your history go?"

"We don't have history in your sense," Fly in Amber said. "Your history is a record of conflict and change. We have neither,in the normal course of things. A meteorite damaged an outlying area of our home 4,359 ares ago. Otherwise, not much has happened until your radio started talking."

"You have explored Mars more than we have," Robin Hood said, "with your satellites and rovers, and much of what we know about the planet, we got from you. You put your base in this area because of the large frozen lake underground; we assume that's why we were put here, too. But that memory is long gone."

"Some of us have a theory," Red said, "that the memory was somehow suppressed, deliberately erased. What you don't know you can't tell."

"You can't erase a memory," Fly in Amber said.

"*We* can't. The ones who put us here obviously could do many things we can't do."

"You are not a memory expert. I am."

Red's complexion changed slightly, darkening. It probably wasn't the first time they'd had this argument. "One thing I do remember is the 1950s, when television started."

"You're that old!" Jain said.

"Yes, though I was young then. That was during the war between Russia and the United States, the Cold War."

"You have told us this before," Robin Hood said. "Not all of us agree."

Red pushed on. "The United States had an electronic network it called the 'Distant Early Warning System', set up so they would know ahead of time, if Russian bombers were on their way." He paused. "I think that's what we are."

"Warning whom?" Jain said.

"Whoever put us here. We're on Mars instead of Earth because they didn't want you to know about us until you had space flight."

"Until we posed a threat to them," Dad said.

"That's a very human thought." Red paused. "Not to be insulting. But it could also be that they didn't want to influence your development too early. Or it could be that there was no profit in contacting you until you had evolved to this point."

"We wouldn't be any threat to them," Jain said. "If they could come here and set up the underground city we saw, thousands and thousands of years ago, it's hard to imagine what they could do now."

The uncomfortable silence was broken by Maria Rodriguez, who came down from the quarantine area. "They're done now. It looks like all the kids are okay." She looked around at all the serious faces. "I said they're okay. Crisis over."

Actually, it had just begun.

12. THE MARS GIRL

Which is how I became an ambassador to the Martians. Everybody knows they didn't evolve on Mars, but what else are you going to call them?

Red, whose real name is Twenty-one Leader Leader Lifter Leader, suggested that I would be a natural choice as a go-between. I was the first human to meet them, and the fact that they risked exposure by saving my life would help humans accept their good intentions.

On Earth, there was a crash program to orbit a space station, Little Mars, that duplicated the living conditions they were used to. Before my five-year residence on Mars was over, I was taken back there with Red and three other Martians, along with Howard Jain, who would be coordinating research.

Nobody wanted to bring them all the way down to Earth quite yet. A worldwide epidemic of the lung crap wouldn't improve relations, and nobody could say whether they might harbor something even more unpleasant.

So I'm sort of a lab animal, under quarantine and constant medical monitoring, maybe for life. But I'm also an ambassador, the human sidekick for Red and the others. Leaders come up from Earth to make symbolic gestures of friendship, even though it's obviously more about fear than brotherhood. When the Others show up, we want to have a good report card from the Martians.

That will be decades or centuries or even millennia—unless they've figured a way around the speed-of-light speed limit. I'm pretty confident they have. So I might meet them.

A couple of days a week, the Elevator comes up and I meet all kinds of presidents and secretariats and so forth, though there's always a pane of glass between us. More interesting is talking with the scientists and other thinkers who vie for one-week residences here, in the five Spartan rooms the Mars Institute maintains. Sometimes rich people come over from the Hilton to gawk. They pay.

The rest of the time, I spend with Red and the others, trying to learn their language—me, who chickened out of French—and teach them about humans. Meanwhile exercise two hours a day in the thin cold air and Martian gravity, and study for my degrees in xenology. I'll be writing the book some day. Not "a" book. The book.

Every now and then some silly tabloid magazine or show will do the "poor little Mars Girl" routine, about how isolated I am in this goldfish bowl hovering over the Earth, never to have anything like a normal life.

But everybody on Mars is under the same quarantine as I am; everybody who's been exposed to the Martians. I could go back some day and kick Dargo Solingen out of office. Marry some old space pilot.

Who wants a normal life, anyhow?